SPELLWEAVER

Ann Crawford

Published by Lightscapes Publishing

Distributed by Bublish, Inc.

Cover by AM Designs Studios

ISBN: 978-1-948543-21-7 (paperback)
ISBN: 978-1-948543-26-2 (eBook)

For

Betsey

my sister by birth and by heart

Scotland

1597

SECTION ONE

EARTH

CHAPTER 1

I loved her more than life itself. And I killed her.

I was not the man who came to snatch her away from us, nor was I the man's disgusting, servile toad-eater who lit the fire under her with such a look of glee on his face. I might as well have been, though; because I didn't stop it, I killed her just the same.

But this was a woman who couldn't be killed. Truly. You could take the life from her, but you couldn't take her from Life, for once she lived here, the world was never to be the same. Oh, just imagine a woman who is so in love with living, so in love with the break of each new dawn, so in love with her body, even so in love with the very air around her. For that's how she moved. That's how she glided through her day, that's how she danced on the hillsides, that's how she bathed under a waterfall, that's how she slept, that's how she ate. It was like she was making love to the water, to the sky, to her nighttime dreams. And how fortunate was her food to be chosen by her — to be turned into such a life and, ultimately, such love. It was like she was making love to life — every minute of her day, every minute of her too-short life.

And I took that life from her.

Oh, did I love her. I didn't know that love could kill anyone. I thought only hate did that. But I loved her so much I killed her. When she was taken, I thought I would regret it for all of eternity.

I suppose you might want to know her name. Catriona, it was. Beautiful—just like her. Beautiful, passionate, alive Catriona. Yes, I realize that anyone on the planet and still taking breath would be alive, but Catriona put the true meaning into the word. Alive. Aye, she was here to live. She was living the idea Life had when we were first imagined into existence. Unfortunately, so many people on the planet while still taking breath are so far from alive.

I promised myself I would never let such a thing happen again. Life, give me one more chance, and I would set it aright. I would help someone else live. I would sacrifice myself. And aye, I had all those chances. Sometimes I remembered, but more often I didn't. And I'd ask for another chance, and another…and I'd be given that chance, and another. Life is very accommodating that way.

Nay, but this isn't a story about death and misfortune and having to come back to right wrongs. It's a story of life and its very celebration. It's a story of what true love really looks like.

Catriona reached her hand out, closed her eyes, and held her palm over the cluster of herbs. She hovered for a moment or two until her hand was drawn to one particular plant. She opened her eyes and smiled at the herb.

"Remember, ask permission before you take one," she instructed her sister. "They always say yes, of course, but still you must ask. You cannot take what is not given freely, or the power in it will not work. And let them tell you which one to ask. Some are more ready in the moment to be used than others, aye?"

Catriona snapped the herb and placed her hand over the break for several seconds without waiting for a response from Elspeth; there would be none. Once she felt the break in the plant would heal quickly, she placed the herb in her basket. The two women moved to the next cluster of plants where Catriona repeated the steps.

Elspeth did not talk. Ach, she seemed to understand her world around her for a few moments, here and there, but then she would retreat into her own sphere again. Picking plants on the gentle, rolling hills with her beloved older sister was one of the rare times that she was in the outer world fully, albeit silently.

"Just imagine the perfection of a world where there is a healing balm for every single thing that could ail us," Catriona smiled.

People of our village say that Elspeth chattered and babbled when she was a baby, but she stopped when her mother died. As Catriona assumed the mantle of mother in addition to being her older sister, their father retreated into himself. Elspeth never had to say a word to Catriona, because her sister always understood the meaning behind every look. We villagers did not know if that was a good thing or not, because Elspeth never had to learn to talk or communicate clearly any other way. And only Catriona really knew what she was saying.

"Want to see the colors, Elspeth?"

After her sister's eager nod, Catriona put her hands over Elspeth's closed eyes. She breathed from her heart into Elspeth's heart and then allowed the energy to flow from her hands into her sister's eyes. She slowly pulled her hands away. Elspeth kept her eyes shut, dancing with the vibrant rainbow of swirls in the suddenly glorious, enchanting world behind her eyelids.

Colors. We'd see a pale, grey-yellow winter sunset. Catriona would see it warmed by red and amber with multi-colored prisms shooting through it. We'd see ominous dark clouds overhead, and she'd see silver and blue and gold and purple. We'd see brown mud, and she'd see the colors of the flowers coming up in the spring.

The only thing we saw in myriad colors was her hair. It lit up the village! Ach, it had every color of the day's sunshine in it—from a crimson sunrise letting us know that the rains were on their way, to the scarlet sunset, letting us know that a beautiful day was coming on the morrow. It had the golden strands of a clear, high noon and the silvery strands of the clouds rolling in. It glowed like the sun itself and waved on her head like the grasses blowing in the gentle winds. Blended together it was like a shimmering golden-red curtain or a red-hued flow of gold. It cascaded down her back to below her waist, and unlike most of the other women of the village, she did not care to tie it up and away, pinned at the neck. No, she let it blow in the breeze.

It seemed like the sun followed her around, all though the day, residing in her hair, her eyes, her being. Perhaps it kept one special ray on her, for she seemed more lit up than…well, more than anyone, really.

Neither sister had any clear memories of their mother, for she died less than a year after Elspeth was born, shortly before Catriona's second birthday. She'd had complications in childbirth, especially since the second had come so soon after the first, from which she never recovered. Catriona did not hold this against Elspeth, but their father did. He took to hating his younger daughter, he took to his bed, and he took to his drink. The villagers would see him stumble out his door for his first time of the day when the sun was past its zenith. The crystal clear, sky-blue eyes that both of his daughters inherited became red and clouded over with despair. His once robust build and attitude became stooped and frail.

In his prime he was the leader of the village; later that title was in name only. His drink was his true leader. We let him believe he was still in charge, but the other elders made decisions, and then let him think they were his idea—"Oh, that was a great idea you had, Edward; we put it into action." And we carried on the way we thought best.

Surely this—well, both of these things: the physical death of the one and the emotional death of the other—must have effected Catriona, but you wouldn't have known it. Where she learned to be this way was a mystery to us all. It was like she was tapped into some special planetary pulse, maybe a spring that delivered a special elixir. Maybe she partook of some special brew. I don't know. None knew. None could explain it.

I don't mean to imply that Catriona was a saint. It was not like that. On a bad day, and she had a few, she could let many a froward utterance fly forth from her mouth. She couldn't sing, neither, although she never let that stop her! So nay, she wasn't the high priestess of the hills or anything like that. She was just a regular woman who decided to make her life so much more than regular. A woman who took an ordinary life and decided to make it anything but.

How she learned to make that decision, we didn't know. We didn't know that anyone could make such a choice. Ours was a beautiful, yet brutal world; an abundant, yet punishing existence; a fecund, yet grueling reality. So many in our time and place chose to focus on the "yets" of that time and place, the time and place of our lives. It was beautiful, yet…. The land was rich, yet…. We had enough food (usually), yet…. We could find love, yet…. We didn't know any other way. But somehow she knew.

We'd hear her talking on the hillsides when no one was near her. "Who are you talking to?" we'd ask.

"Oh, many," was her frequent answer.

Whoever they were, they were Life's whispering of secrets to her. Many of you say in these days, "I didn't get the handbook." She received the handbook. We didn't know then that it was simply a decision she made.

What was special about her wasn't anything in particular that she said or did—only in how she was. Somehow, one would feel different after she walked by. Better. Like the day's burdens had been lifted. Like the sun was suddenly shining a little brighter and the day was more vibrant, or the moon was more silver and the night had become more mystical. Even if she was hungry, as happened often as winter was on the wane and spring had not yet arrived, her face wouldn't betray any discomfort. Even if the rains kept us all inside our tiny cottages for days, which they did on frequent occasion, she'd emerge like she'd just gone inside for a quick, refreshing nap. We didn't know what to make of it. She had some connection to….something. Even now I can't explain it. Back then it was like she had received a special message before arriving on this land, like she had a royal or papal dispensation for special privileges. Aye, she should have been born in a castle with servants to serve her meals and draw her bath. But here she was in our tiny village near the edge of civilization, where our mighty mountains met the heavens, where our mighty Scotland ended abruptly to meet the endless waters. Her little cottage was just like every other of the near two dozen little cottages in the village, but she treated it like that castle she should've been born in. Wherever she went, whatever she was doing, the land seemed to rise up to meet her.

Ach, but our land was so beautiful. I hope the kings and the popes enjoyed their lands as much as we did ours. Mountains surrounded our village, although the peaks spent much of their time cloaked by the clouds. Ah, but when the clouds lifted, oh, I don't think Heaven could have been any more beautiful than those green mountains, radiant emerald in the summer sunshine, amber in the other seasons, with the blue sky offering a promise of eternity. On those clear days we would climb the highest mountain—"our mountain," we called her—to gaze into the distance at the high cliffs crumbling into the sea, which was still a day's walk away. A salty stickiness was delivered to us from time to time via the winds. We had nothing to compare our scenery to, only the stories of travelers passing through, but we thought none in the world would be finer than our land. Life wasn't easy. I mean, we didn't know any other life, but when the hunt returned nothing, when the crops failed, when winter lasted longer than it ought, we were still grateful. Aye, for our land, although not much else, we were grateful.

There was one in the village who despised her, but only one. And he despised her for the most despicable of reasons—he wanted her and couldn't have her. She wasn't to be had. Shane envied her—body, mind, and spirit. All of us did. We all wanted to be her, to see what it was like to live inside a person who cherished the day, who embraced the raindrops as much as the sunbeams, who embraced the night as much as the day, who embraced the darkness inside a person's heart as much as the love and light that lives within us all.

He followed her to the hills day after day, year after year. She was always smiling, always pleasant, but never sharing of the treasure he thought he wanted from her. She did share one large treasure, though—she would successfully steer the conversation away from the darkness in his heart.

"Did you see the sliver of moon setting o'er the far mountain?"

"Nay."

"Gives me such a full, peaceful feeling in my heart."

He wanted the peace in his heart without having to look at the moon. Of course, looking at the moon was not what gave it to her. And she wasn't telling him about gifts delivered by the sighting of a sliver of moon—only the possibilities that availed his own heart if he'd just allow them to.

But she smiled that brilliant smile—aye, men have killed over such smiles, even some not near as brilliant—and disappeared into her home.

"Ach, Shane," we'd try to persuade him again and again, "you can't possess a rainbow."

"You can't hold on to laughter."

"Aye, you can perhaps capture a bird, but what you have in your hand is not the freedom and splendor that you fell in love with when it was up in the sky."

He'd scowl at us and then disappear for hours. And then he'd follow her up the hill the next day.

We could never speak aloud who introduced Catriona to the plants and their healing properties as well as their healing energies — all things we weren't supposed to talk about when strangers came to the village. You just never knew who was who nor what was what. We heard agonizing stories — for instance, one time a man arrived at a village just a three-day's walk from ours and said he was a healer. That gave all the women in the town an opening to tell him their healing tales and remedies. And he had them all killed.

Those were awful times for being a woman, for being a healer, for being different, for being a person who loved God but not as the Church dictated we were supposed to love God, Life. Many of these stories were included in the history books; even more of the stories were not.

The thing we could never explain, even though we tried for years and years afterward, is why we let it happen. But anyone who tried to stop those atrocities was assumed to be guilty, too. What a choice! Try to stop them from killing your beloved and be killed....or not try to stop them and let the guilt and the dreams of what could have been kill us all in the end anyway?

But it was just one man, one man and his obsequious, oafish, dim-witted, stunted servant—a toad-swallower as you heard me refer to him earlier. In my day, at least in my days in that particular life several centuries ago, sometimes a charlatan would swallow a toad so that some professed master, a street magician, could then "save" him. You know the word as *toady* now. This young wretched man was the epitome of a toady.

We all saw the toad-swallower that way, except for Catriona. We all hated the witch hunter, except for Catriona. The whole town could have risen up again them, after all it was just two men—well, one and a half. That other strange being could hardly be called a full man. But we knew, even if these two disappeared into a nearby loch, more would come. And more after that. And....

He was the true weaver of the spell, not she, and he put us under it. The witch hunters were the ones with the real black magic. Meanwhile, witches heal. They don't kill people.

He came with the fortress of the Church right behind him. In our gentle town in the valley, far from the men who formed the church, he came with some kind of authority that we could not—well, did not—question.... for reasons that still, even when regarded from the other side of life where things oftentimes make more sense, did not make sense. Being dead doesn't mean we agree on it, over here in the afterlife—oh, no. To tell you the truth, we argue over here as much as we did over there. It's just that here we laugh about it so much more, but I can't really laugh as I'm relaying this story to you.

From this side of the veil—the other side of life from where you are—we see how fleeting and temporary life on Earth is. So taking a life isn't such an enormous deal, not in the wide spectrum of things. But it should be on your side. You cannot speak a word of hate without damning your own self. You cannot even think disparagingly of others without condemning yourself to what you're thinking about them. You certainly cannot take a life without darkening your soul. It's like life is a web, where everything is connected, all is one. And it's like life is a small pool of water: if you think of a brilliant aquamarine, the pool turns that color; if you think of dark grey, the pool turns that color, too.

During those times the witch hunters were among those with the darkest souls of all. And the darkest souls were looking for one thing and one thing only: the ones with the light.

CHAPTER 2

Always, Catriona was the first to awaken, long before dawn. It was her favorite time of day. The messages from the nighttime dreams were still whispering to her, although they had a serious contest of being heard between the heavy breathing from Elspeth, who slept beside her, and the raucous snores from her father across the room. She knew that her mother especially used this time to relay messages. She could sense light beings still hovering in the air around the bed.

After a quiet visit to the bucket behind the screen, she stole back to the warmth of the bed. Like the evening before, she put her hands to excellent use. She rested her hands on her heart; sometimes she put one hand on her belly, sometimes on her throat, sometimes lower down on her body, sometimes over her forehead, sometimes on the crown of her head. Always, one hand remained on her heart. After a moment or two, the pulsing began. It was as though her hands became fused to the part of the body they were resting upon, as though she couldn't move them if she tried. She could picture the light of her hands connecting to her body of light. So much for "Remember man that thou art dust"; at least one of us remembered that we're made of stardust. And as for that "and to dust you will return," nay, we return to the stars.

Catriona was rarely ill; nor were her sister and father. If her herbs didn't heal them, her hands would. It was unfortunate she couldn't heal her father's love of the drink. Perhaps she figured that that's what kept him alive, perhaps the pain of living without that particular buffer would've been too much for him.

Elspeth awoke next, and she'd snuggle next to her sister, relishing the extra radiant warmth provided by Catriona's light work. As their father's snores slowly subsided, the two women would brave the morning chill and dress and revive the fire. Elspeth handed their father his morning meal, as Catriona was wont to let her be the heroine whenever possible. Try as both would, though, nothing could really assuage his anger at his youngest, his grief at his loss, his resentment at life. Interesting that he lived with such a bright light in his own home, but never let it shine in the dark corners of his soul until it was too late.

The girls would eat as quickly as possible and then do their favorite chore of the day: head to the hills. Rain or shine. Winter or summer. Actually, we can scarcely call such an enjoyable activity a chore.

Just like the day before, and the day before that, Catriona gave her sister lessons on the herbs. Surely even through Elspeth's simple headedness, she would've known the lessons by this time, but the two enjoyed the words. The words were a balm, liturgical—like they were a daily mass. For Elspeth, tiring of her sister's lessons would've been akin to tiring of a meadowlark's song.

When the sun was high overhead, they'd start to turn back.

"Oh," Catriona said, "I forgot one herb, a necessary one for old man Cameron's poultice."

Elspeth nudged Catriona in the special fashion that signaled one thing: Shane was near.

"How's Shane today?" Catriona sang out.

Shane never saw Elspeth give the signal, so he must have assumed Catriona had eyes in the back of her head.

"We'll be here for a while yet, so we'll meet you back in the village, aye?"

He hesitated, but took her cue. Instead of heading back to the village, however, he walked further up the mountainside.

"Yes, my love," she said without looking up to meet Elspeth's look. She knew the glare was there, however. "I've told you before. My words are not an invitation. I've done everything I've thought of to do — I've put a sphere of love around me, I've put on an armor of light, I've put up shields of metal like the warriors, but the only way to truly ward him off is to give him what he's looking for. I bring him straight into my heart. I give him love. And then he's satisfied for a bit and not flitting about like a moth at a candle."

Elspeth's expression registered that while she was not happy with her sister's actions regarding this man of the shadows, she understood.

After making the midday meal — and letting Elspeth serve it to their father — Catriona would leave for her rounds, her sister in tow. First was usually old man Cameron who was so old even he'd forgotten when he was born. He was always in need of something or other, or perhaps it was just their company. His own family was so fatigued with his babble that they left long 'ere he was awake and returned long after he was asleep. That's a slight exaggeration, but not much. They'd feed him. But Catriona would talk to him, and the sisters would listen to his stories—aye, although only for about ten minutes and then they'd proffer their excuses for rushing off. He lived for years under his healer's care, far longer than he would have otherwise.

Next would be the newest mother in the town and her babe in arms. There the sisters would linger as long as they could. Who could resist the joy of new life? Certainly not them. Few women died during childbirth in our village, not with Catriona and the elders who taught her at hand. Unfortunately, that seeming miracle and good fortune for most new families made the girls' father's pain all the much harder for him to handle.

Following the newest mother would be anyone else who was ill or in pain. At some parts of the year, that would mean returning home well into the night, although Elspeth would run to her cottage to give their father his evening meal and then return to Catriona's side.

For all his faults, Shane never pretended to be sick to try to attract Catriona's attention. But Aileen did. That young woman came up with more imagined ailments than most of us combined. More about her story later.

If the number of her charges allowed for it, Catriona and Elspeth would join their father for supper, and then they'd head to the cottage wherever the night's entertainment was taking place. Singing, musicmaking, storytelling—ach! We couldn't imagine the royal jesters and troubadours being better than our folk when it came to making the groups laugh, join in the singing, dance to the fiddler's tunes.

Somehow the weariness of a day of farming or tending to the sheep or whatever our chosen tasks were dissipated in the evening's revelries. This is how our small village stayed so tightly woven together, despite the many disputes that would inevitably arise. So how did….ach! More about that later, too.

Not all would attend the evening's festivities, of course, which was good because no cottage would fit such a crowd. In the summertime, when the skies were light well past the usual bedtime hour, we'd gather in the town square and there the gatherings would be larger.

Some nights the menfolk would come together in their own circle, as would the womenfolk. The laughter would rise to the stars from the cottage that the men were gathered in. At times the same happened for the gathering of the women, but more often they were much quieter, more reflective gatherings. The stories of childbirth, the mysteries and secrets that accompany womanhood — we, too, shared the teachings of the wisdom of the ages passed along since time immemorial. We, like our ancestors, shared messages around hearths that have burned like that since the beginning of human time.

Like many of our ancestors and human relations we didn't know — siblings by other parents — some of us could see, hear, touch things outside our own realm and we'd relay those messages. We'd touch the earth and relay the messages from the Mother of us all. We'd stare into the scrying bowl and let the water speak her magic. On summer nights we'd lie under the stars and speak to the air, to the vastness above us. On winter nights we'd stare into the fire and let the dancing flames speak to us of other times and places, other realms and dimensions.

Catriona would be quiet during these times, allowing the elder women their opportunity to speak. And often all of us would be quiet, just cherishing the company of women.

When she'd finally lay her weary body down for the night, Catriona pulled a circle of her "many" around her. She didn't know who they were, apart from her mother whose energy she could definitely distinguish from the others. But she did know they were there for her. She'd often awake in the middle of the night feeling she'd traveled far, and she'd know she had more travels ahead of her before her predawn rituals. We all travel afar in the dreaming time. Most of our evolution/growth/work happens then; few know that. She did.

CHAPTER 3

We could spy a visitor long ere he—and it was always a he—arrived in our tiny village. The pathway down the mountain was in plain sight of 'most everyone's walkway in front of the tiny dwellings that all met up with the two dirt paths that comprised our town…that is, unless it was raining and the clouds covered our mountain, in which case few would be standing in their walkway anyway, and even fewer would be coming down the mountain pathway.

But such was not the case on the day Byron came to town. We saw him walking down the mountainside a good twenty minutes before he arrived. Oh, he was handsome—we could tell that even from so far away. He had brown curly hair that hung to just below his shoulders. He was a strapping, young fellow, barely into his twenties. As soon as we saw him, we knew who he would be with on Beltane, if he stayed so long—which he would if he had any sense to him.

A group of us met him as he walked into the village. Catriona was still in the hills, but we knew it wouldn't be long before they met.

By the time a visitor arrived in our environs, his food rations were bare. It's quite interesting that there was such a huge expanse of land between us and the next village. We humans could spread ourselves out and each have a home with a large parcel of land to call our own. But nay, we prefer to clump together, from the small clumps of tiny villages like ours to the large clumps of the big cities we'd hear about from the many travelers who passed through. We don't know how so many found us, but every month would bring one or two travelers. Some came from as far away as London and some had traveled even farther than that. It was beyond what any of us could imagine, and not that many of us left to go see for ourselves. We were quite content with our tiny village in the valley, nestled between three mountains. Seeing the mighty waters from atop the mountains was good enough for us. We didn't have to go to them.

"Welcome," William, one of our elders, boomed out to our visitor amidst the cries of greeting.

"Hello, hello. Thank you. I'm Byron," the stranger announced to the questions swirling around him.

"Where do you come from?"

"Near Glastonbury."

"Glastonbury! How long have you been traveling?"

"Almost a year," he answered.

Aileen grabbed him by the arm and steered him to her cottage. "Well, come to our home. You look famished. We'll make sure you're filled up to overflowing for the next leg of your journey."

Aye, that's our Aileen. Every town has one. She was a beauty and on her own accord would have stood out far and above the other lasses—in any other village. Not ours, however; just her luck.

There were always ninety-two of us, it seemed. When one was born, another one died. When one set off on a journey, a stranger arrived and stayed. We had twenty-three thatch cottages that housed at least two, sometimes up to six, although that high count was never for long. As you already know, of course, Catriona and Elspeth shared their father's home. Shane lived with his parents and younger brother. Aileen lived with her parents and brother and sister. Our little crowds kept things warmer in the cold times—aye, perhaps too warm as tempers would flare when we've spent a little too much time with each other.

It was one of those beautiful spring days that would make even the most cynical person on earth have hope for the future. We were in very strange times. Perhaps many times are strange. It's strange to hang someone on a cross, it's strange to behead someone, it's strange to light a fire under someone's feet. To take a life is the strangest thing of all and yet humans do it so readily, easily, and often.

Strange how we had just emerged from the "dark ages." But in so many ways our age was still just as dark.

But on that day, all those things seemed very far away. With nary a cloud in the sky, the sun warmed the soil, and the heather and grasses swayed gently in the breeze.

Byron politely extricated himself from Aileen's clutches, with the help of several men from neighboring cottages who called from the dirt path in front of her cottage.

"Come, tell us of your travels."

"What news can you share with us?"

"We have more food for you if you're still hungry."

They walked him to the square—it wasn't anything formal, really, just some slabs of rock in the center of all of the cottages. It was more of a circle.

"You are most kind," Byron said.

"To rescue you from Aileen's clutches? Yes, we're very kind to do that," William chuckled, but quietly since Aileen was not too far away, following the group, obviously despondent that her food offering and allure hadn't kept him longer.

Byron's smile relayed that that's exactly what he'd meant. The murmuring in the square drew the rest of the villagers from their homes, and all of the residents, from our eldest elder to the youngest babe, was in a tight circle around him. Travelers were our only source of news.

"Tell us what you know."

"Have you heard that Queen Elizabeth—" But he'd glanced up at the hillside where Catriona and Elspeth were walking down the pathway. The royals of far-off London were instantly forgotten as our local royal was spotted. Catriona's wall of hair shimmered in the sunshine. She was talking intently to Elspeth and had not yet noticed the entire village watching, waiting. In fact, it was Elspeth who noticed, and she nudged her sister.

It wasn't unusual for all of us to be gathered together. Actually, we needed nary an excuse to be as one group, especially on a beautiful day. But Catriona's eyes immediately rested upon the stranger in the center of our circle, both human and symbolic.

She actually stopped. Not much swayed this lass, not much at all. But this time she stopped.

No one moved. Nay, there was one who left: Aileen. But for the rest of us—ach, you think we were going to miss this? We didn't have books and movies. We didn't have many real-life romantic stories. We had wind and weather and crops and births and deaths and, aye, even weddings with dancing and singing and blushing brides and all. But we rarely had the opportunity to witness the very moments that fairy tales are written about. No, not often.

What could have been going through her mind? What was she thinking? Aye, here was a young buck far more handsome than any our village had to offer, but it was more than that. When I passed from this world to the other worlds, I knew. She'd been with him before. She'd be with him again. And at that moment, her entire being —body, mind, spirit, heart, crown, radiance—remembered him.

Ach, at the time, we even knew, too, although we didn't know that we knew. What we did know, clearly, was that Beltane wasn't going to wait for these two.

How did she make it past one hundred and seventy-six eyes looking at her—of course we couldn't count her own, Elspeth's, Aileen's, or those of the two babes—without seeing a one of them? The only eyes she saw were his.

"Let's see about hunting some pheasant for supper, shall we?" called out Catriona's father, who hadn't had much to drink yet that day, surprisingly and fortuitously, and who probably could feel grandchildren in the offing. We didn't stand on ceremony much. We were also a nosey bunch, which comes when you don't have much new to feast the eyes on. But we dispersed, albeit very reluctantly, to let the fairy-tale moment unfold without us.

Elspeth hesitated, not quite certain what to make of this new situation. Her father took her by the hand and led her to the burgeoning garden before he took off with the other men on the hunt. Fortunately for us all, he was a clearer version of himself that day.

Two human beings were coming together, but it was a special coming together of two pairs of eyes, two hearts, and two minds. (Ach! I could not resist watching from the doorway of my cabin, as many of us were.) I could practically see strands of light and magic pulling these two together....but their eyes had a mystical power all their own.

His luminescent brown eyes spoke of worlds yet unseen, of voyages to be taken. They showed an embrace of life, a willingness to experience it to the fullest.

Her blue eyes spoke of wisdom beyond her years, of knowing things from other realms, but of staying in one place, of being completely grounded and connected to the earth. Earth met the sky in her eyes.

A yearning for adventure, wanting to touch, taste, smell, soak up the entire world is what his eyes bespoke…wanting to lie on the earth and feel the pulse of humanity…to speak foreign tongues, to drink exotic concoctions, to engage in new rituals. Whatever it was he was looking for would be around the next turn, over the next hill. It was the journey that was his calling, not a destination.

She wanted to plant herself here, in one place, forever…to go ever deeper, yet higher at the same time…to feel the planetary pulse from here, without having to go searching for it. It would come. Everything does—everything. She knew she just had to show up first and make herself available to it.

The two spoke long into the night. The fading stars finally urged them to their beds...where they didn't sleep.

Early the next morning, William took him for a walk, and just happened to go by Catriona's house. Three times. Everyone knew she was the earliest riser. Where could she be?

We didn't know that she'd already headed to the hills. She watched William walk our visitor around the little village and past her home — all three times. She'd gone to quell the strange palpitations in her heart. Aye, she knew this was the man of her late-night dreams, the one whose touch she'd felt many an early morning. She knew it was her destiny. But still, the palpitations needed quelling.

Finally, after an hour or so of no movement from the little cottage, William glanced up the mountainside. When his eyes finally rested on glistening copper, which would've been Catriona's hair, he practically shoved Byron in her direction.

"Why don't you take a walk up the mountainside and see if you can find something for our dinner?" He left before Byron could even answer. But Byron looked where his host had been looking, and was rewarded with a view of spun copper, as well. He started up the mountain.

Catriona met him partially down the mountainside. Perhaps she'd wanted to make it look as though she was foraging for greens instead of just sitting on the hillside watching him and quieting her heart.

"Hello."

"Hello."

The entire world disappeared as the two wracked their brains for words to come after that one. But nothing was in either brain. So they laughed, always a good releaser of tension as well as a time taker. And they laughed. And laughed. The eighty or so of us who were watching were scratching our heads. What could possibly be so humorous?

And then they walked farther up the hillside. They disappeared into.....what? There was no mist or cloud cover that day. But disappear they did.

They walked in silence for many minutes. Finally a complete sentence formed in her brain.

"How long have you been wandering?"

"A long while."

"More than one year's time?"

"Aye." His somewhat complete sentences were not quite as complex as hers. Someone from the Glastonbury region might not have answered this way, but he'd been in our parts for many months.

They sat down on a soft patch of grass in the middle of a grove of trees. Another complete sentence occurred to her to articulate. "What is it that you are seeking?"

"To sail the seas, to taste all the world's spices on my tongue, to hear as many foreign words on as many tongues as I can. To be the adventurer."

"But you already are what you're seeking. That's usually true in mind, but with you it's also true in life."

"Aye. But I need to taste those spices."

The two were silent for several moments, lost in their thoughts. They watched their world around them. The same wind that was gently rustling through the tall grasses was gently pushing the clouds toward the mountains, bringing with it a scent of the salt waters from many miles away.

"So why did you come this direction? We don't have many spices in these parts, last I knew."

"Perhaps because I was seeking you first of all. I just didn't know that when I set out."

Byron placed his hand under her chin and drew her face to his. The surge that electrified her entire body from the mere touch of his mouth on hers was beyond anything she'd ever known. Did lightning just shoot from the heavens through her and into the ground?

"Catriona."

Did he speak that aloud or did she hear his heart calling her name? He gently leaned her back until she was lying on the ground. His face was momentarily lost in the brilliance of the blue beyond him. As he leaned in to kiss her again, she took note of every curve, every line, every inch of his face.

She loved the smell of him: His scent was like…brown. If colors had a scent, his would be this one: of the earth, soaked by a passing rain cloud and awaiting more coming rains; like the trunks of trees; like leather. Her hands caressed his strong shoulders, his strong back.

When his mouth was complete, for the moment, with its exploration of her mouth, he started kissing the side of her neck.

"Maybe I don't need those spices after all," he whispered. "Nothing in this world could be better than the taste of you."

"Nor you," she whispered, trying to catch her breath and calm her racing heart.

She knew Shane was lurking in the shadows of the trees, and she didn't care. Even if the two weren't hidden by the tall grasses when they were lying down, she knew things would not proceed much farther than this, with this complete stranger…this complete stranger she'd remembered all her life and perhaps from lifetimes past and perhaps even from lifetimes to come.

She knew time could bend upon itself. She looked into his eyes and saw the man she had been with so many times, and remembered from the future the man she would be with again. And again.

"I knew I was seeking someone; I just didn't know who," Byron said, interrupting her memories from the past and the future. "I knew you were alive and going about your day and singing and laughing. I just hoped you weren't married yet. I knew you'd be beautiful and full of light with dancing eyes and laughter that sounds like bells on the wind."

She laughed, ringing the bells, as if to bring his words to life. "And I knew you'd be strong and handsome and adventurous. I just didn't know how….." He looked over at her as she paused. "Adventurous! And strong and handsome," she quickly added to his crestfallen face. "I was teasing, my love."

He took her in his arms. Then he proceeded to pretend to take a bite out of her neck. "Mmmmmmm. Very tasty."

"Have you tasted many necks along your journey? Perhaps one in every village along the way?"

"Oh, at least. But none so delicious."
"You say that to every lass."
"Just those with a neck."

They sat for hours more, not saying much, but volumes were spoken. He, too, seemed to be remembering every line, every curve of her face as they gazed upon each other — this stranger they'd known forever.

As the day waned, they wandered up to the top of the mountain, where they could see the mighty waters

"Aren't you ever curious?" Byron asked. "Don't you ever want to see…oh, what's on the other side of that hill? Or beyond that sea there?"

"No. Maybe in another lifetime."

The sun was starting to reach the waters in the West.

"We'd best be on our way," Catriona sighed. "Where is it you're staying?"

"Aileen's, I think her name is."

"Ah, of course," Catriona laughed. "But not after you've spent the afternoon with me, you won't. She'd sooner pour scalding liquid over you."

"Perhaps…..your home?"

"Nay, I'm sorry. We don't even have room for the three of us, and no extra beds. But I'll find another spot for you."

As they headed down the hillside, Byron started to speak and then stopped himself. And again. And again. "How did you get so wise? Up here, by yourself, I mean."

She laughed, and his heart opened even further at the light, airy sound of bells on the breeze again. "Ach, you don't see a wagon full of wisdom lying around that I would've picked up?"

It was his turn to laugh. Her heart opened, as well.

"Aren't we all so wise? Don't we all have a special wisdom to call our own? Aren't we all so talented and special in our own ways?"

Byron shrugged and then commenced his starting-to-speak-but-stopping-routine again. "You've heard that there are men coming to small villages to…well, to…hunt…women."

"Aye, of course I've heard that."

"Especially those who heal."

She flashed a smile at him.

"And especially those who smile like that. Those who don't seem afraid of anyone or anything."

"And when I'm asking for a bed for you, how long should I tell the family you'll be staying?"

"Don't try to change the subject!" He sighed. "A couple more days. Maybe more," he added quickly, to the crestfallen look on her face.

"You will stay for Beltane of course?

"Of course."

She smiled. "I'm happy."

"Not as happy as I am."

The rays of the setting sun lit up her hair to match its crimson hue. Her eyes matched the cerulean blue of the sky behind her. Never before had he seen a woman so beautiful, nor would he ever again. Ever.

Never had she felt the love of life personified in one person so magnificently, nor would she ever again.…at least not in that lifetime.…but theirs was a love to continue in other places, other times.

Ach, every man in that town committed adultery in his heart every time he saw her walk by.

Aye — and some women, too.

Hush, you'll have your turn.

Aye, we squabble on this side of the veil, too.

But that longing stopped that day as most realized, in some recesses of their souls if not in their minds, that the love reserved for this golden lass was beyond what any of them could offer, let alone comprehend.

Of all the gifts humans have during their many, many lifetimes, finding true love is the greatest gift of all. Love of another human being is the way to express the infinite love in all its glory. It puts music into form. It finds harmony in a caress, sunshine in a glance, ecstasy in a touch.

Love. Finding what can be such an elusive, chimerical, ephemeral quality that has such a hold on people but can evaporate like a dream in morning's first light — ach! It's rarer than the most precious of jewels…the reasons wars are fought…the reason nations are built. For a fortunate few, it lasts years, perhaps even decades.

For some, it might last just a few days, but it's enough for that lifetime.

Ann Crawford

SECTION TWO

WATER

Ann Crawford

42

CHAPTER 4

Nay, it wasn't the previous storyteller who killed her. It was I. I turned her in. I sent a message that brought the hunter to our village. I don't think he ever would have found us, tucked away in our hamlet, if it hadn't been for that message.

I'd say that I would regret it for all of eternity, but I won't. Ach, I thought I would when I was there. It tormented me until the end of my days, which came surprisingly soon after Catriona's. I helped my days end far sooner than they might have otherwise. I didn't think I could bear that pain for days more, let alone another forty years or more.

This side gives far more understanding to such events. But I won't excuse myself. There was no excuse for what I did. None. I hated life. I hated her. I hated her for the life she had—the livingness within her, not the life she happened to be living in, because our physical existences were quite similar—same small village, same customs. But while the rest of us were bound by the constraints of those times, she lived in a freedom of her own making.

Ach, nay, I didn't hate her. I loved her more than life itself, too. And I couldn't have her. No one could. She wasn't someone anyone could "have." I thought I hated her, but what I hated was the sight of someone living a life that was so full, so alive, right in front of me but that I couldn't live.

I could have, really. Anyone can live that life. Many do, more and more. She gave of herself with such abandon. We were all so closed, so cloaked. It never felt as though we had enough energy to make it through the day. The skies were always so grey, so oppressive. There wasn't even enough love to share. We didn't know how to tap into that inner spring that she had somehow discovered. How she did find it was a mystery. Not so much now as we know it's available to all, all the time.

There's a freedom that comes from giving so much; the freedom comes from knowing that the more you give, the more you have. The more you have, the more you can give. And then the bigger the treasures of the spirit are. The circle goes 'round and 'round, creating more love, more joy, more to give, more to have, more to give. But I didn't know that then.

She did have a love before Byron, but it was a love of heart and not of body. Catriona and Thomas were the same age. You'd think they were twins, the way they moved through life as a synchronized pair. The two spent their childhood entwined in each other's day, arms, lives. As a child, the mornings would find Catriona running hand in hand, with Elspeth. Elspeth tired easily and would sleep much of the time between the midday meal and supper. In the afternoons, her hand would be locked in Thomas's, as the two ran through the hills.

As the sisters and Thomas grew into their teen years, Elspeth grew stronger and Catriona realized that her sister was her primary responsibility; close behind was her responsibility to gather herbs and help heal anyone who was ailing. When we weren't gathered as a cluster of the town or as a gender group, she and he would gather.

They'd lie in each other's arms watching the stars, talking into the wee morning hours.

One time I listened in. I don't think they knew I was there, but you never could tell with those two—her especially. Shane wasn't the only one who thought she had eyes in the back of her head.

"What do you suppose is beyond that star?"

Bah! I didn't even care what was beyond our nearest hill. So much for that. I didn't eavesdrop on them after that—well, not often, that is.

There was something slightly different about Thomas, but we couldn't put our finger on it. Whatever it was, it didn't bother Catriona any. I should've figured it out at the time, but I didn't.

Maira, the oldest woman in our village, was the one who taught her about the plants and herbs. Maira was also the wisest person in our village until Catriona reached age, oh, eight perhaps it was. Even Maira could recognize a wise elder when she met one, even if the elder was six decades younger than she.

Maira was as close to a mother as Catriona had after her mother died. She tried stepping in to the role for Elspeth as well, although no one other than Catriona was ever certain what Elspeth was thinking, and no one but Catriona could fill that role for the younger one. Maira lived with her sister, Siusan, so Catriona and Elspeth had a surrogate aunt as well. Actually, Maira and Siusan were not sisters but they were so old that the other elders couldn't remember that the two weren't related and the younger folk never questioned it.

But Siusan was Maira's lover. The villagers thought their husbands died ages before and left them alone. Who was going to bother two old widows whose children had left them as well? Truth be told, they never had any children, but the other elders seemed to forget that, too, and the younger ones, aye, never questioned it. Actually, the two women never said an untrue word about their life circumstances. People just assumed they were widows and that their children had left long ago. Interesting how sometimes a tale can develop without a word being told.

Catriona sang the arias of her heart to the hillside as the sisters carried their armloads of kindling back from the woods to the village. It was a good thing Elspeth didn't care about much, because as the first writer told you, Catriona could not sing well—at all.

"Ach, Elspeth, are we allowed to be this happy, when so many are suffering so?"

Elspeth's smile answered the question.

"You're right," Catriona smiled back. "It's what we're supposed to be. It's what we came here for."

Catriona and Elspeth dropped their bundles of sticks by the hearth. While Catriona set the fire, Elspeth swept the cottage with a broom comprised of a long branch with twigs and moss tied to the end. After filling the kettle with water from the jug, Catriona carefully hung it on the hook over the fire.

The evening meal was a luxurious fare: roasted rabbit, which Catriona had thanked profusely as it died from a heart attack in her snare, plus roots, bread, and milk.

She brought half the meal to Maira and Suisan, as she generally did.

"Gracious, Catriona. You shouldn't have." Maira gratefully took the basket.

If Catriona didn't bring supper time after time, the two old women might've gone hungry. At their age, they couldn't hunt, they couldn't garden; nay, they could barely bake a loaf of bread. But they could remember the teachings of the ancients, and they could pass those on. And they did.

Most of our cottages were dingy and dank. The stench didn't bother us so much, as we were used to it and didn't know any other. If you walked in our homes, however, you probably would not hesitate to make your excuses to leave. But a few of the homes — Maira and Suisan's as well as Catriona's to name two — smelled like herbs. Somehow they always remained fresh like the morning air after a cleansing from the overnight rains.

Catriona did not linger with the elder women as she usually did. They did not mind. Theirs was a solid love for life, but it had long passed from the sparkle and spangle that the younger woman suddenly found herself in.

"How long is the young man staying?"

"Not much longer."

"Ach. Oh, that he would stay."

But even the old women knew it wasn't meant to be that way.

The water coursed down the mountainside, over some large rocks, and into a pool. Catriona stood on the rocks under the fall and let the water tumble over her. The frigid water made her head tingle and body shiver, but the sun was unusually warm on her bare skin, which made the ice-cold water more tolerable than usual.

The clear-blue sky gleamed above, and the air over the pool magically luminous as the drops of water caught the sunshine. But she was the main thing shining.

Ach, here was a woman so comfortable in her body, so at home in the flesh—more so in that one very moment than many of us experience in an entire lifetime. She was grateful for her slender, yet still womanly, shape—the soft swell of her breasts, the gentle curves of her hips, her long legs.

So many of us were taught to loathe our bodies, to think upon them as made of original sinne, as dirty, as somehow ungodly. The only ungodly thing about them is the thought of them as ungodly. The more godly idea of the body as the temple of the soul has spread around the world now. But, actually, the soul is far, far larger than the body. The soul houses this beautiful structure that carries us from place to place as we do and give our....specialties.

Everyone is special. Everyone does something special that outlasts his or her life.

She sensed the eyes watching her from the brush, but she didn't care. People can only steal what they ultimately feel does not truly belong to them, and if the gift is freely given, a theft cannot take place. Besides, here was her glorious body, one of the most divine gifts of life. She would have preferred going without clothing all the time, but the chill of the land forbade it, let alone the protestations she would encounter.

She ran her hands across her belly, over her breasts, up her neck to her face and through her hair.

Her ablutions were made all the more precious because they were for him—not the him who was lurking in the bushes near the falls, but the visitor to our village. Byron had become quite the celebrity with us all, regaling us with tales of his travels. The fair lasses didn't even attempt to gain his attention, however; they knew he was smitten.

"Maybe he'll stay and they'll marry," one lass said to another. "That way the next visitors will be fair game for the rest of us."

"It is rather tiresome to never have a whisper of a chance with her around," the other responded.

Specific customs about Beltane varied from region to region, even village to village. It started as an homage to the coming harvest. Too much or too little rain would yield a small harvest, and we'd suffer the following winter. In days long 'ere ours, a man and woman would come together in lovemaking as an honoring of the greatest harvest of all—human life...and in hopes that the harvest would be good that year.

Some enclaves were puritanical in their approach to life and so were the same in their approach to Beltane. Our village could be fairly puritanical in many respects, but for Beltane we let all decorum fly on the winds. We built an enormous bonfire, wore masks, and did....whatever we wanted, with whomever we wanted—as long as the wanting was consensual.

To many of us, Beltane was the main holiday of the year. We celebrated the joys of the flesh with wanton glee. A year's supply of pent-up lust was released. Those who had no partners had a partner — or two or three or four — on that particular night. With leaves, bark, and dirt masking our faces and the darkness of night masking our bodies, we could be anything or anyone we wanted to be, if just for that night. Oh, to celebrate the magnificence of the body in all its splendor, to celebrate the magnificence of the sense of touch in all its glory....

Some thought it was wretched, a sinne, a horror. When they'd state their opinion, we others would politely suggest they stay home and shield themselves from this part of the celebration.

We could hear each other in the woods and on the hillsides in the throes of lovemaking, and it expanded our own arousal. If you think about it, separate homes and walls were invented a very short time ago. For millennia our ancestors made love to each other in front of each other. Well, perhaps it wasn't quite on open display, but certainly near each other. It was natural. This part of life is a natural part of life. This is how life re-creates itself. There are few forces as mighty and powerful as this one. But many didn't understand it. Many feared its power, so this sacred side of our true nature was rele- gated to the darkness...and the darkness within us rose to counterbalance that. You know of what I speak. How many politicians and men of the cloth — and people in general — rail against the very thing dark thing that they do, or are?

Nay, no one *is* dark.........but turning from the light of life can darken the inner light. And when the inner light is diminished, the misery is so unbearable that they have to find others to participate in the dim world of falsehoods that they create. And humans are such a confused bunch that many do choose to participate. Ach!

The flames twisted and twined, leaping at the pitch canopy overhead. The joyous screams and calls echoed off the mountainsides.

As she walked through the meadow, Catriona put a screen, a cloak to make herself invisible, around herself until she saw him. She didn't want to have to turn down the others — and there would be many to turn down.

Their eyes met across the bonfire. A shooting star wouldn't have arrived at her side any faster than he did.

He took her hand and gently kissed it. She ran her fingers down the side of his face. How many times had she seen him in her dreams? Finally, she was able to touch the man of her heart.

They walked off into the darkness together.

Ach, how do I describe a first union in the flesh after so many in the dreams? Perhaps it's like waking up to find yourself in the middle of a rainbow? Nay, in a lightning bolt? Is it like walking through a fog all your life and suddenly the clouds part and the sun's light evaporates the remaining mists?

Certainly she'd touched and been touched by many. But they were all preparing her for this night, this moment, this man, this touch.

He picked her up in his arms and spun her around several times before gently setting her on the grass. Electricity shot through her body as he softly ran his hands over her hair, her face, her body. He picked up her foot and kissed it, then kissed her lower leg, then her upper leg, her torso. Their lips met and the electricity surged ever more. Almost of their own accord, their bodies joined in sacred union — one being, one motion.

As he came to completion, rapture exploded inside her womanhood. Flames climbed the inside of her being and burst out through her hands, her feet, her heart, her throat, her forehead, and finally through the top of her head — her crown.

Lying in her state of ecstasy, her senses were heightened beyond compare. Her body felt like it was shining as bright as the sun. If she opened her eyes, would she see herself lighting up the nighttime skies? She could hear and feel the earth breathing. She could sense the birds sleeping in their nests in the branches overhead. The trees leaned toward each other, bringing their pointy branches together to form a protective shield around them.

But someone had been watching.

Nay, two people had been watching.

Hours passed before they emerged from their magic cocoon and could speak again. "You know I'm leaving tomorrow?" Byron whispered to her.

"Aye."

"Don't let them come for you. Come away with me."

"That I cannot do."

"What keeps you here?"

She didn't answer.

"Your sister and father will be fine," he told her. "And your village will find another healer."

She still didn't respond.

Byron wrapped his arms around her. "Aye, then stay you must. But please leave when they come. Will you?"

Still no words came back to him.

"They fear you," Bryon whispered. "Not just you, but others like you. They fear your power. People like you and me, people who know the great mysteries, are the Church's main competition. If everyone knew we all have power within us, then why would anyone have to look to an external authority like the church....and give it money? But you already know all this. I'm not telling you a thing you don't know. Since the truth is hidden from so many, who don't understand, I can speak these thoughts aloud to very few."

"Aye."

They lay for a long while in silence, holding each other.

"Aye," he whispered at last. "I know who you are, and I can't ask you to leave."

"Aye, I know who you are, and I can't ask you to stay."

He slowly stood and gathered his clothing. After he dressed, he knelt down next to her still supine body, picked up her hand, and kissed it. "I'll wait for you."

She looked up at him, puzzled for just a moment until the deeper meaning of his words dawned on her. "It won't be that long, my love," she replied.

"Until then." He disappeared into the darkness.

As she lay motionless, still relishing the sensations of their lovemaking flooding her body, one of the watchers came out of the darkness. Shane stood over her and then tried to lie on top of her. She pushed him away.

"It's Beltane," he hissed at her. "You have to."

She pushed him off her and jumped to her feet. He started toward her again, but she held up her hand, warding him off.

"Shane, you can have anything you want, any time, if love is your invitation."

He grabbed her, pushed her to the ground, and climbed on top of her. With all her strength, she tried to push him away but failed.

No, her mind screamed, this could not be possible, especially not after the warm, bubble of love she had just been in. This was beyond comprehension. This was just intolerable.

For the first time in her life, she willed her spirit to leave her body. To her utter amazement, her inner self rose from her physical form. She watched from a short distance away.

It's just a body, she assured herself. *They're our bodies, the results of the lives we lead, but they're just dust of the earth after all. The real me is over here, where I am right now.*

Shane looked into her eyes and saw her utterly vacant stare. He shook her, then raised his arm to slap her.

Catriona's spirit self watched him closely. He didn't just want her body, he wanted to possess her, to own her, to be inside this body that contained so much light and joy and power and freedom—qualities he could not imagine possessing for even a moment, let alone a day or a lifetime.

Realizing the futility of his motions, he stopped and rolled off of her. Catriona returned to her body and arose. With compassion in her eyes, she quietly said, "There are far greater ways to have the feeling you desire."

He pushed her to the ground and disappeared into the night.

And the other person watching? Who had the fortune of watching true love and then the misfortunate of watching love misdirected? It was I.

An attempted rape is not something anyone would want to watch, to be sure. From the beginning of this particular act involving these particular people, however, the power was not with the rapist…the would-be rapist, that is.

I was tucked away amongst the trees, watching the actions unfold. I was as in love with Catriona as Shane was, if love could be used for such a twisted emotion in both of us. We actually didn't love her then. Hate wouldn't be a more appropriate term either. It was an intense yearning to…well, we would not have called it such at the time, but we wanted to feed on her. Our own lights were so far suppressed inside, but we had a vague awareness of our true possibilities when we looked at her.

Not knowing any of this, I thought I hated her. When she was killed, I was glad. Or so I told myself at the time.

Long hours in the middle of many a sleepless night informed me otherwise. During the day I could keep busy with the chores. But nights always brought me back to myself and the truth.

I thought my guilt was because she was a woman.... and so was I. That kind of love wasn't allowed then. But really, that had nothing to do with it. She was everything I wasn't. She was so very happy; I wasn't. She was so very beautiful; I wasn't. She was able to find love everywhere; I wasn't. I wasn't able to find it anywhere. She had life; I didn't. I wanted hers.

When I was dying many years later, she took me her in golden wings and helped me cross over. At least that's what my imagination told me at the time. I know better now, of course. But it was a lovely easing out of a fairly loveless life...of my own making.

The power garnered from having been with him was winning over the tragedy of losing him...at times. Her body would flood with joy at the memory of him and being with him—in body, mind, and spirit. Then as the next moment reminded her that he wasn't there any more, her body would flood with the loss.

For several days after Beltane, Catriona took to the hills from early morning to late night. There weren't many who were sick at the time, so the only one who really missed her was old man Cameron. Elspeth was with her, of course, but gave her sister the time and space she needed. She communicated with the herbs in her own way as Catriona sat with her eyes shut, remembering.

On the third day, the two descended from the hills as the sun was about an hour from setting, practically blinding them with its brilliance.

What was that? Was that the sunlight playing tricks with her eyesight? Was it magick that brought this apparition? Or....could that really be him standing there?

All questions were hushed as he took her in his arms. Sobs of joy and relief overtook her. She held his face, still not believing that this was him, this was her beloved Byron. He picked her up in his arms and spun around with her. Her arms locked around his neck and her face buried in his chest as he carried her to a grove of trees on the far hillside.

No one watched them go — nay, no one. We all had far better things to be doing than watch fairy tales unfold again. (Aye, that was to say that most of us were in the village circle, coveting their moment and good fortune.)

"I couldn't leave," he whispered as he set her down on the grass. "Not yet. I walked as far as the sea and then south to the nearest port city. But I had to return."

"But that's many days of walking, there and back. You must have angels' wings on your feet."

All words were hushed as his mouth met hers. Together again, they breathed as one being. One entity took in the oxygen; one entity expelled it. One heart was beating. There was one flow of blood.

He was over her. The motion of everything slowed down. A bead of sweat ran down his forehead and nose and....stayed there. She was riveted, mesmerized by this drop of water from inside his being. It contained the entirety of the cosmos, a universe in miniature — as did every cell in his body, and her body, and every cell, every atom everywhere.

This was far beyond physical — the whole of her being merged with him and the whole of creation at the same time. As their internal love exploded, a scream escaped from her mouth — a pronouncement that here in this place of exquisite ecstasy, in this heart-opening moment, her body was embracing all of Existence, microcosm meeting macrocosm. The pinnacle of human sensation was meeting the summit of the sublime.

Long after her screaming ended, she lay gasping for breath. Energy streamed out of her hands, feet, and the top of her head as the warm, pulsating throbs slowly subsided. She had merged with the ground. In the arms of her lover, she melded and became one with him, too. She had merged with the divine, as well, but was the loving, grateful, holy, mystical mistress of the physical... that incredible sensory experience that we embody for... that gorgeous gift of life and physicality that so many take for granted or, worse, shun.

She turned her head and her eyes rested on the blades of grass next to her. She saw the entire act of nature in each one of them: the sun, the rain, the minerals in the soil.

An insect crawled along the blade of grass and she saw the miracle of life. That's all miracles are — life looked at with the eyes of love. Everything is a miracle.

That's what love does: it shows us the entire cosmos within one entity. It blasts open the heart to see the beauty, the majesty, the...miracle.

She was more in love with life than she'd ever been. Falling in love with this beautiful man just opened her even more — like the galaxies opening to the universes.

Yet love was such a small word to use to describe such a vast feeling. Her heart was cracked wide, wide open. It was expansive, a cosmic connection. It was a communication with every atom in all of the All. She saw shapes and forms and colors folding over on themselves and emerging in new shapes and forms and colors. Shadows of ancestors long gone and descendants from far into the future passed before her.

She looked at Byron and witnessed a metamorphosis before her. First he appeared as a very young child; then she saw him as a lad, then a young adult, then the magnificent man that he was, and then…it stopped.

She had seen this before. She would watch a young child playing in the lane outside of her home and watch the years come upon the child, as she transmogrified into a wizened, old crone, with all the ensuing, in-between years crossing her face — the young woman, the bride, the young mother, the matriarch. She'd see an old man and see his life spinning backward to the robust man he'd once been, then the raucous youth, then the wee child.

She tried to see Byron as the old man that he would be some day, but no vision came. Instead he came back into focus — the stunning, smiling man before her.

He wrapped his arms around her. Nestled together, they drifted off to sleep.

The rising sun warmed her skin. Catriona ignored it because she knew that as soon as she opened her eyes this glorious, warm sphere of love and light she was in would evaporate. He knew she was awake, but forestalling the inevitable. He took some strands of her hair and tickled her face with them.

"Not yet," she whispered.

"Aye, my love. I'd best be going before long."

"I can think of a way to delay your departure."

After they made love in the early morning sunshine, he kissed her and then rose. She knew this was the final good-bye—for this lifetime.

CHAPTER 5

Catriona placed her hand on her belly as she walked down the hillside. She'd known within moments of his departure that there was a part of him inside her body as well as inside her mind. It all had happened so fast; in addition to being a symbol of him, the growing life inside her was a sign that it all was real, not a dream.

Her mind's eye brought him to her: he was on a ship, making a crossing over very rough waters. She could practically feel the sky's grey chill in her bones and the ocean's spray on her face. But she could also feel the warmer destinations that lay ahead for him.

It had been a long, long walk, but she was almost home now.

"Where have you been?" her father asked her.

"Trying to catch some food on the far hills. But twice night came upon me too quickly and I had to stay."

No one ever doubted anything she said. While few of the other women in the village would take to the hills by themselves, let alone for a night or two, she would. But, while we didn't know this at the time, she'd actually been on an important scouting mission.

Catriona listened for her father and sister's breathing to fall into the steady rhythm of sleeptime. Somehow she needed very little sleep, compared to the rest of us.

Since Byron's visit, she would quietly leave the little home, wrapped in her shawl, and head a little ways up the mountainside. She'd set out her shawl and stretch out under the canopy of stars, if the clouds allowed for it. She felt as home in the heavens as she did on the earth. At least once a week or so she'd fall asleep and awaken to either the streak of light in the east or the raindrops from the clouds that came whilst she slept.

She was motherless certainly, and fatherless, too, to an extent. The very ground beneath her and the canopy of the sky overhead had seemed to become her parents over the years. She didn't have the language to describe the expanse above her. We did not talk in terms of infinity and eternity much—it was more than we could fathom.

She also felt the earth stretching far beneath her. At that point we'd heard stories from many a traveler who spoke of sailors who did not fall off the edge of the world, but we had no concept of how large our planet was—let alone that it was a "planet." So, to her, the space above her and the earth below her felt to be about the same distance. And it did not matter to her.

As the first storyteller told you, nighttime was when she'd come alive. Sometimes her dreams would bring scents of flowers—flowers she'd had no connection with in that particular earthly existence. But I know now they were gardenias. She dreamed of angelic beings bearing messages, and although the exact words would often fade in the morning light, she could feel the messages imprinted on her soul. Her "many" were with her always, but especially in the darkness.

One night, before she spread her shawl out before her, she paused. She became aware of a strange, new, exciting energy filling her entire being, and beyond. The energy in her feet suddenly went deep, deep into the ground while the energy in her crown soared beyond the clouds. Her body felt like a shimmering column of light, with every inch of her being—physical and etheric—dancing in ecstasy, buzzing with aliveness. The energy rushing from her palms was magnetic, hot, almost fiery. She bent over and touched the earth, aware of the mother's heartbeat deep within the planet. She became aware of her own luminosity.

She lay down on her wrap. Every night when she shut her eyes and before she went to sleep, she put her left hand out, palm up, beside her on the bed—receiving. She put her right hand over her heart—giving. After just a few moments of streaming, as she called it, her body would be a circuit of energy and her right hand would fuse to her heart. She couldn't move it if she wanted to. Energy streamed through her and out of her. She was never quite sure what she was doing or what was happening, but she knew it was a gift—to her and to the world.

Catriona did not have words to put to most of the numinous experiences she had. She tried to explain some things to Maira, but even the older woman, despite all of her wisdom, had not tasted anything like her protégé spoke of.

She'd hear many a mystical tale from travelers passing through the village. But she never said anything of her experiences to the minstrels and troubadours, just took in their accounts of seeming miracles. Many a traveling minister had come, hoping to impart the gospels and the word of the Lord to the villagers, but they never stayed for long.

More and more these days, when Catriona did finally fall asleep, her dreams would be filled with even more beings from other realms—the light realms, the angelics, other worlds, perhaps from the stars. Sometimes the beings were from other parts of this world—she'd awaken from time to time with the smell of gardenias lingering, or many another flower that lived far from the Scottish hillsides.

Have you ever watched the sunrise? Of course you have. But did you ever receive that special message from the very first ray of light that shoots over the horizon? If you've never been privy to that singular sonnet, meant just for you, perhaps you could try it sometime.

Shortly after sunrise brought Catriona's own special message, the clouds rolled in, bringing a chill. She sighed and headed home, wrapping her shawl tightly around her.

Her bleeding had stopped for four months and her belly was starting to protrude. Her heart sounded an alarm—and the message from the first ray of the sunrise that day confirmed it—telling her to let no one know.

From the instant she felt life inside her womb, mere moments after Byron left for the last time, she knew she was having a son. She talked to him in those mystical hours before sunrise, and she talked to him during those magical hours after sunset. During the day's chores at home and around the village she'd sing as she always did, but no one knew she was singing to a certain being in particular.

She envisioned him as a babe with Byron's enormous brown eyes, as boy with Byron's long curls, as a man with Byron's broad, strong shoulders. She pictured him wandering the world like his father, finding love in the nether reaches of faraway lands.

She cried more than usual in those days, not only from the hormones shooting through her, but also from the knowledge that she wouldn't see very much of his life, at least not in the physical. She regretted the pain that his young life would endure. But as with the loss of her own mother, the pain of her loss would temper his soul, form his spirit, be the texture of his life to lift him higher than he would otherwise have gone. One of the highest blessings of losing her mother at such a young age was learning that she'd be all right no matter what else came her way.

Pain is a high honor of this life, your life. (Yes, we're dodging those etheric eggs and tomatoes you're throwing at us.) But human life is designed to experience the full spectrum of emotions. There are many places in the universes where that is not possible.

When the pain is so severe that you feel you can't go on, when you are lying on the earth wanting to give up and become one with the soil, to go to a place where the past is not even a distant memory....the earth is holding you. The elementals are guarding you. The angelics are rocking you in their arms. The celestial realm is beckoning with its finger, pulling you forward, ever forward

And you are envied. You have a body. You can feel that full spectrum of sensations. Do you know how much of creation is not in physicality? A very small percentage of all that is, is actually matter. An even smaller percentage has senses to feel, touch, see, hear, taste, experience. anything, let alone so much of it. All of it.... in doses.

Some folks come in knowing that they are only here for a short while. Perhaps they come just to teach those of us who are here for the long duration how to best live our lives. How could she not be scared or sorrowful? She was; but she also knew that life here is only a mere snippet of the whole and she let herself be carried by the invisible realms.

If she was so knowledgeable, so sure of her place in the whole of things, why did she even bother? Why did she stay? Why would she come again after? There are other places where she'd be a neophyte; there are other places where some (whom you'd never suspect—you know those seemingly insane people around you, aye even those in your politics) would be the wise masters.

What do you do with those who seem to have found the secret, the answer, the resolution of the mystery? In those days, we killed them.

Aye in days of old and in your days, too.

Catriona laughed more, too. Not only were the hormones surging through her, light and love were, too. Perhaps she was just all-out living more, although she was doing that before Byron and her babe came into her life.

One rainy night she stayed in the cottage, but didn't sleep. What was she seeing? Her eyes were closed and the new day had not yet dawned, but it was as though the sun was shining on her eyelids. She opened her eyes to see if a torch-wielding intruder had entered her home, but the room was black, as before. She felt a sphere encircling her body. She breathed to the outer edge...and back in. And out to the edge...and back in to the center of her being. She heard a thrum—was it just her ears throbbing, was it the thrum of the planet, was it the thrum of the welkin, the celestial bodies? Her body was vibrating, buzzing like the busiest of bee hives. And at the very center was the queen, ever patient, peaceful, silent, awaiting the goods delivered on her command.

She gently massaged the crown of her head, which seemed to have developed a life of its own, even more vibrant than the life dancing in every cell of her being. She held her palms up to the darkness over her, knowing, just knowing that light was streaming from them. She opened her eyes and was richly rewarded: a soft light emanated from her hands.

A small cry broke her reverie: Elspeth, just awakening, had seen the light, too. Catriona quickly put her hands on either sides of the younger woman's face and kissed her forehead.

"My dear sister, my dear, darling sister—that's what we're here for." She kissed Elspeth's forehead again and brushed away the tears that were slipping down her sister's cheeks. "That's what we're here for. Yes, my love, we come here, we discover people and animals and flowers in the sunshine and hills bathed by moonlight and the solid ground beneath us and the bigness overhead; we fall in love, we have babies, we dance in the meadow, we sing to the angels, we wake up, we light up the world. What we're here for is to feel this aliveness, this oneness with all. It's so rare to have this feeling, this knowing. But it's right here, all the time."

Her rush of words dissipating, she rocked her sister back and forth, back and forth in the darkness.

"If for nothing else, to have this knowing for one single moment, is why. What. For." She wasn't even sure what she was saying, but she was heard, felt, and understood by her sister...and by the whole of creation. "This very moment. This one."

One flower blooming, alone on a hillside, never seen by anyone, lifts up the whole. One heart blooming, alone, lifts up the whole. One heart blooming that can show another heart how to bloom, lifts up the whole, and those who are touched will never be the same. And the whole will be forever changed, never to return to the former way of being, because the igniting will continue without end.

One morning as winter's warning was in the air, leaving well before dawn, Catriona and Elspeth both carried blankets attached to packs of clothes and provisions on their backs. They walked and walked and walked—up hill, down hill, over dale, even stepping through streams. "We're setting off on a new adventure," Catriona told her sister. "You like new adventures, my dear sister, don't you?" Elspeth shrugged. "Father will be fine," Catriona insisted, addressing the unasked question in her sister's eyes. "Yes, of course we'll be missed, but we won't be gone very long."

Many a traveler had told the villagers of the cave high in the mountains, as it was a perfect stopping point for a night's rest. Catriona had heard about it so many times that by the time she and Elspeth arrived there, the sight of it felt familiar.

But Byron had mentioned another cave a little farther away, one which the villagers would probably not venture to look for if any search parties were sent forth. Had he foreseen her requirement for a hiding place?

Nothing about him and his knowledge and the events he could see would surprise her.

This cave, too, was well used by travelers, but not by those who ventured to her village; instead they followed the path to another village in the region. Tucked into a crevasse, which would help keep the winter winds to a minimum, it also afforded a nearby opportunity to see if anyone was coming for miles in three directions. The mountain behind them was extremely jagged, steep, and snow-covered, so no one would likely be coming from that direction.

Right near the cave's opening sat a good-sized fire pit, and at the back of the stone dwelling was a hole dug for sleeping. Several large stones had been placed around the hole in an attempt to keep drafts off the temporary residents as they slept.

They were fortunate that both women, the tiny Elspeth especially, did not have large appetites, but with a third being to feed, Catriona wasn't sure how much more hungry she'd be. The mountains provided much food in the form of numerous rabbits and red squirrels. Catriona had also been smoking extra meat and setting aside food since the days of the longest sunshine.

The women built fires only at night, so the smoke would not draw any attention to their location. During the day, when they were not hunting or gathering firewood or spending the couple minutes it took to straighten up their encampment, they put on every piece of clothing they had and clung to each other for more warmth.

On many a dreary, rainy afternoon, Catriona and Elspeth would stare out the opening, mesmerized by the drops falling. Catriona would watch the drops slither down the stones around the doorway. A single drop, joined by another, inching slowly down, taking their time....then joined by another and the whole mass of drops would quickly slide down the rock to the ground. Strange how fascinating things can become when not much else is going on.

But much was going on inside. Catriona would take Elspeth's hand when the baby would kick and move. Much was going on inside Catriona's mind, as well. The rains often kept a cloud cover so she couldn't watch the heavens, but at night when she shut her eyes, she'd see stars shooting, galaxies swirling. At night and sometimes during the day, too, the wind would howl incessantly, sounding like cries and moans.

Sometimes when she couldn't sleep, she'd brave the cold and sit in the cave's entrance, watching the skies. There was a star cluster that would command her attention, but when she'd look at it, it would disappear. She'd look away and see it appear out of the corner of her eye. The experience was strangely compelling. She could tell that some of the whispers around her were messages from that star cluster, but she couldn't hear exactly what they were saying.

Where do we come from, she'd wonder. Do we come from this ground beneath us? Do we come from the fearsome God of the church after all? Nay. Perhaps we come from the stars? There was someone—another sister, a daughter, a mother, unquestionably a female—who knew her and was watching her, waiting for her to return. It wasn't her own mother, who watched her from her special place beyond the veils. This other had a different feel: vast, ancient, loving beyond measure, even beyond the measure of her own mother's love. Perhaps she hailed from that alluring star cluster.

One day as Elspeth shook out the bedding at the doorway to the cave, Catriona arrived with a dead rabbit, thinned out by winter.

"That should tide us over for a few days, anyway."

As on the first day of their journey, she responded to the question in Elspeth's eyes. "We can go home soon." And to the next question in her sister's eyes, she said, "Soon is, well, in a bit. We have to stay here for a while. But you're going to have a baby to play with even sooner than that. You would like that, would you not?"

There were no more questions in Elspeth's eyes, only homesickness.

"Do you want to see the colors, my love?"

Before Elspeth could even respond, Catriona covered her sister's eyes and breathed from her own heart into Elspeth's heart and streamed energy from her hands into her sister's eyes. When she pulled her hands away, Elspeth was quiet, lost in the soothing world of the colors.

The sisters watched the snow fall, mesmerized by the magic and peacefulness of the gentle swirl of flakes. Dancing, swirling, sometimes moving upward on a surge of wind. The tree branches sagged under the weight of the snow. Momentary whiteouts occurred as the winds picked up.

As the flakes fell, she almost felt as if she was rising. Although she sat in the shelter of the cave's entryway, she could almost feel a frosty brush on her cheeks as the flakes touched the ground.

A new world appeared before their eyes. Fresh, clean, a new start. Just like every night. Just like every new year. Just like birth. Just like death.

Her swollen belly was taut against her garments, scratched by the coarse, woolen fabric. It wouldn't be long now but it couldn't come soon enough.

Nighttime fell, and the two retreated to their beds. But she couldn't sleep. So she spoke with her son, her beloved child: *Welcome to this world. You're going to be a strong, powerful man of peace. You're going to see things I've never even imagined, have children who will have children who will have children who will see and do amazing things.* She heard an answer in the affirmative.

She lay with one palm up, one palm down on the bare dirt, breathing in sync with the rhythmic pulse of the planet. Wait, was she breathing or was the earth breathing her?

Catriona never wanted for much, and yet she received so much—so much more than most ever dreamed of. She never seemed to need what most people would want—comfort, warmth, luxury. It was like she wasn't of this world. Maybe she wasn't.

But she was. Perhaps she was the right idea of this world...a fully alive human.

Or maybe she was a harbinger, of a world of the future—after humanity stops its arguments over who was right, who owned this land, who was going to hell.

There is no hell. Everything is what you make of it, here and in the hereafter. But we can't judge anyone for their beliefs, either. What if what they are believing, right now, is what their souls need for their evolution?

What if everything you've ever thought, ever wanted, ever did brought you to this moment? This place? This time?

What if that's just right?

74

CHAPTER 6

The townspeople gathered in the center circle. The figure in black had been descending the mountainside for near on to an hour, but still seemed far away. A smaller figure in black stayed to his heels, much like a dog.

We knew his presence was bad long ere we saw his face. A dark cloud clung to him and his minion. Dour. Sour. Looking for meaning in the wrong places. Finding some where none existed.

By the time the man and his attendant arrived in the village center, only a few of our folks remained. The others, with a distinct sense of dread, had scattered. The village dogs growled at the pair.

"Welcome to our humble town," Catriona's father said.

"Yes," said the younger of the two.

Strange response, even from one so strange. He didn't seem to be much more than a boy, and one look at him would tell you that he hadn't been given much intelligence back when they were handing it out to the group that came in when he did. His mouth was set in a perpetual sneer, and his eyes danced with some kind of demonic glee.

The older man seemed ageless, although he must've been into four decades, at least. He had obviously taken part in the sinne of gluttony, which must've been quite gluttonous when he had the opportunity, given that he'd just walked —

"From London," he told the group when they asked. "Not directly from there. I've strayed from the path here and there as things called my attention."

There was an empty cottage right then, which was very unusual, but deaths and marriages and in-laws moving in sometimes took their course. We thought it very fortunate at the time, as surely no one would want to be a direct host for this pair...but perhaps it wasn't so fortunate, as things turned out.

Catriona kept a familiar. You call them pets, now. This cat would follow her like a puppy and keep her eye on strangers like the fiercest guard dog. With her mistress gone, the cat was even more on alert.

As the small group from the square led the two to the cottage, they passed Catriona's house. The cat hissed at the man, arching her back with all of her hair standing on end.

"Who lives here?"

"The man who greeted you in the square. Plus his two daughters. One is quite simple."

"And the other?"

"Just a regular woman. The two sisters disappeared last autumn."

The man gazed at the house for a moment. "She'll be back."

Catriona stared at her hand as it grasped the wall of the cave. Oh, it seemed alive and apart from her, apart from this pain that was tearing out the inside of her body. She tried to suppress the screams but couldn't.

"It's alright, Elspeth," she comforted her trembling sister. "It's alright. I'll be alright soon."

She stared at her hand again. As another wave of tremendous pain washed over her, her hands clawed at the wall, trying to find something to hold on to.

Elspeth handed her a piece of clothing to clutch.

Her body felt like it was ripping apart. Oh, how could tremendous physical agony be such a normal part of life? And how could any woman choose to do this over and over again? For a short while she forgot all of her training in the healing arts. She forgot her connection to her body. There was only the searing pain.

Then she remembered the reason for this pain: This beautiful being who chose to come through her—quite literally at this moment. He was the doorway of the past and the future, where all the potential lay. He'd carry Bryon and her and all their ancestors into the future.

The little being made his entrance just then. As with the multitudes of women before and the multitudes to come after, the pain was quickly forgotten as the warm, wondrous cocoon of love, awe, and nurturing filled her body and surrounded the two of them.

The man walked by the little house and continued down the street. He stopped, looking back at the house.

Catriona took the rag Elspeth handed her and dropped it in the pot of warm water her sister had prepared. She gently washed him.

Him. Her son.

She smiled at Elspeth, who was lost in amazement as she stared at her nephew.

"Would you like to hold him?"

Elspeth shook her head.

"My love, it's impossible to do it wrong. It's the first nature of human nature to care for those who come next. Here, I'll show you how."

As Elspeth took the infant, Catriona fought back tears. "Elspeth, you have to promise me something."

Elspeth couldn't take her eyes off of this living, breathing miracle.

"Dear Elspeth, we must tell everyone he's your baby. You must let everyone think he's yours. Promise me."

But Elspeth was still riveted by this tiny human in her arms and didn't heed the words and the warning they conveyed. Catriona let a few tears fall. There would be time to say these words again…but not much time.

Catriona and Elspeth wended their way down the winding trail, not far from the village. They'd intended to make the trip back in one day, but were unable to. The cold from the previous night lingered in their bones, slowing their steps.

The man had decided not to wait for her any more. As he was giving his good-byes to a few townsfolk in the square, they tried not to appear too delighted with his departure.

From the hillside, Catriona spotted him and stopped abruptly. Elspeth, who had her face cast down as she carefully navigated the path with her heavy load, including the baby, bumped into her. The baby started to wail. Catriona pushed her finger into his mouth, and the cries subsided as he sucked on the pacifying finger.

But a dog barked, and then another. The man looked in the direction the dogs were facing — and then running as they recognized two of their favorite members of their pack.

"Perhaps I'll stay after all," he said.

Catriona gazed at the rosy mouth suckling her rosy nipple. A luxurious, warm peace radiated throughout her body as the baby nursed.

A loud knock at the door broke her reverie and literally lifted the warm blanket of love off of her. She heard the dogs growling outside, and she knew what their protestations portended.

She set Elspeth on the bed with her back to the door, thrust the baby into her arms, and threw a shawl over the two of them. In those terrible times, the children of the suspects were not often killed, but it did happen sometimes. Catriona was not going to take any chances.

"Pretend, my love. Hold the baby there like you've seen me do."

An even louder knock was accompanied by the man's hoarse shout. "Catriona, open the door. I know you're in there."

Catriona finished tying the strings and smoothed out the front of her dress. She looked around her to ensure that the home gave away no signs that she was just nursing a baby. A large wet spot started to seep through her bodice and she threw some water on her. She opened the door.

With disgust, the man and his lackey looked from her eyes to the wetness on the front of her dress.

"Is it now a crime to make a spill when washing?" she asked, pulling her shawl more tightly around her.

The man ignored her and entered the room. Even though her back was to him with her shawl draped around her, he could tell Elspeth was tenderly holding the baby. She didn't look up.

"Who's the father?"

"One of life's mysteries," Catriona responded.

"How could anyone have had a mind to, uh, make her be with child?" he demanded.

"It was Beltane. It was dark. He probably didn't know who he was with. And you can't fault her for that," she said as his eyes darkened toward her sister. "It's a custom in many parts."

Elspeth was lost in a trance with the baby, who must have fallen asleep from his lunchtime feed at Catriona's breast. He wasn't moving or even making a noise, which must have assured the man that the infant was indeed feeding.

The man left…for then. Why did we let him into our lives and our homes so easily? How does such a thing happen?

The healers were known as spellweavers. But he was the one weaving the spell. And we were under it.

Catriona's sleeptime became more active and her dreams more vivid. In one, her body twisted and turned, doubling over itself in somersaults. She couldn't breathe—she put her hands to her neck to try to assuage the choking sensation. When she finally could take a breath, pain seared her lungs. Then all was quiet. Peaceful. She felt her body being swept up in a shaft of light and felt immense....love. A world of love. A universe of love, simply love. That was the only way to describe it. She was surrounded by, floating in, wrapped in, love.

And she was ascending. She laughed out loud and the sound of her own laughter brought her back to earth... somewhat. She was still floating up, up, up.

Catriona awoke as she felt Elspeth's hand on her back, but the dream continued. She almost wanted to ask Elspeth to give her some sign that her older sister was actually still lying on the bed, because she couldn't feel it under her any more. There was only this...love....carrying her upward. She was aware of other souls around her: on either side, over her, under her. Hundreds...nay, thousands...nay, more...all traveling upward, too.

Catriona opened her eyes and saw Elspeth staring at her. She took her sister's hand.

"It's all right, my dear sister. I'm fine. There's nothing to worry about. Nothing at all."

As she drifted back to sleep, she saw him walking toward her. He held wide open for her and she rushed into them.

She'd only seen the great waters from the hillsides— she'd never been close to it. But she could see the waves crashing on the beach and could imagine their mighty power.

The sea had taken him to his next journey beyond this life. But for the moment, he could remain with her, nearly touchable. Their spirits danced. And danced. And danced.

SECTION THREE

AIR

84

CHAPTER 7

Nay, it was I.

I could have...done...been...so much...more than I did...than I was.

Like the others, I didn't light the fire. But I loved her so much I hated her. I hated her so much I loved her. It doesn't make sense because it didn't make sense. I can't explain myself. I was what it was; it was what I was—"it" being the time, the situation, the pain, the confusion.

Shortly after Catriona's return from the hills, twins were born to Gwynyth and Edward. It was a very difficult delivery, but with much thanks to Catriona's midwifery skills, tragedy was avoided.

As she walked back to her cottage early in the morning, exhausted after being with the scared, young mother for almost two full days, she felt the man's eyes upon her.

"Aye, more life comes to the village," she called out to him.

He looked at her blood-spattered frock. "There's no real doctor in the village?"

"Aye." "Where
is he?"

She smiled at him.

A witch knows the healing arts; that's her — or his — crime. She knows that plants have healing properties and knows which ones to use which time. Even the simplest of people of long ago used the plants and herbs with complete reverence. What was revered for millennia, what kept humanity alive for so long.....how could they turn it into a crime?

A witch knows how to hold her hands together to create a fireball of light and power and to pass that healing power on to the ailing one. That power is free and available to everyone. You don't have to believe in a certain God to have it.

A witch is a healer. A witch knows the night holds the mystery and secrets. The moon is her lover and confidante.

Like a sailor learns to read the sky and the winds, and a farmer learns the true lay of the land, a witch learns to read the human body or the world of the plants. But you saw nary a sailor or farmer killed for their crimes. No, they were men, usually, in those occupations.

The women were killed by men who could not have them. They could not have them or have what they had so they extinguished them. The flames that engulfed these women were the flames of anguish that filled these men.

How could they turn sexuality into a crime? In truth, this particular Church was not the first religion to do that — that had been done already…by people who didn't understand, by people who believed in lack.

She set twelve stones in a circle, then sat down in the middle of them. She turned her mind to the quiet realms, where the answers come. After several minutes in the deep silence, she felt a presence...and then another presence... and then another....and then another. She felt twelve beings around her in all.

Catriona did not know of masters of other realms or archangels—at least no one had ever told her about them because she never encountered anyone who knew. But she sensed that there was some hierarchy somewhere, that there were beings working on behalf of those who walk this world. That day she felt the love and light focused on her from these twelve, whoever they were... sent as guides by other unseen beings somewhere.

But why would those beings allow the tragedies of this plane (which you now know as the Earth plane) to happen in the first place? Are there other beings—of the darkness—who are just as strong?

Nay. Satan is an imaginary fiend. The dark side has no darkness once the light shines upon it. How could it? The only thing Earth and the Heavens are made of are light and love. Darkness is made only when a shadow is cast, and the light—any light—eliminates a shadow.

So where were the beings of light when this darkness came to the continent and then to the island nations of the north? Where were the beings of light when the darkness came upon other lands with other atrocities? They were there, too. But life on Earth may be one of the densest of all life anywhere.

Everything is created by thought, and the fear a human possesses is one of the most potent creators in all of creation. It must manifest. Oh, if only we had an inkling of how powerful we are, how magnetic our thoughts are, how vibrantly our vibrations call in our experience.

So if Catriona was a woman of such high vibration, how could she have called in this experience to herself? How could she leave her son, her sister? Why didn't she depart with them to another land?

Because…deep inside…she knew the placement and the timing of things. She had the knowing that life is eternal.

Since she knew her time in this realm was coming to an end soon, it made her open up and soak up the rays of the sun a little more, take her sister's hand a little tighter, and gently stroke her father's cheek a little more often.

I certainly sound wise now, and I was somewhat wise then, too. But I let the vortex of density pull me down to a low, low level.

So many of us want to know more, to be more, to laugh more, to shine more. But when it's right in front of us, we want to extinguish it. It's not hate; it's fear. It's resentment. Here's someone showing us how life could be lived, is supposed to be lived, and we feel we can't do it. Yet. But we're not even aware of that. Yet.

She stretched out on the ground, placing her palms upon the dirt. She could feel the very pulse of the planet beneath her, and even the pulse of the firmament—the sun and the heavens. And there she was, the meeting point of heaven and earth, heaven on earth.

As we've mentioned, at the time none of us thought of the land beneath our feet in terms of being a planet. Certainly it couldn't be something that shines in the heavens like the stars above us. And we certainly didn't know we could shine as brightly or that we were made of the very same star stuff. To us, it was all there was. It was all we knew. And those tiny bright lights far above our heads, shining brightly on nights when the winds swept the curtain of clouds away, well, they were the stuff that poets would write of. But perhaps on rare occasions, those twinkling lights would cause the heart perhaps to skip a beat as some part deep within recognized our connection with them.

In addition to the pulsing beat of the earth and cosmos, Catriona felt another pulsing beat as Elspeth slid her hand under her sister's. Elspeth was loath to leave her sister be when she headed to the hills alone. Perhaps she knew, too, somehow, and wanted to be by Catriona's side as much as she could.

"Elspeth, my love," the elder whispered, "promise me that no matter what happens, you know I love you, that I'll always be with you."

Elspeth's expression revealed that she understood, much as she despaired at hearing the words.

The last supper she made for her little family was a simple fare: rabbit and root vegetables. She served the representative of the generation that went before, the representative of the generation that was to follow, and the one representative of the middle generation that was to stay. She didn't take the leftovers to Maia and Suisan, but left them for her father and sister.

That night, after the baby fell asleep and she was off by herself again, Catriona lay down on the blanket of soft grass. Overhead the stars twinkled at her, on one of those rare windless but completely clear nights. She gazed at the stars for a long while, noticing things she'd never seen before…like that star over there had a red hue to it…and that one that never seemed to move suddenly seemed to.

The night around her was very still, as if even all the animals were listening for her to speak.

"Beloved Life," she started, "Thank you for this day, thank you for this life, thank you for this body, thank you for this land. Thank you for all of it." She felt tears rise and she suppressed them. "I don't know why you want me to leave. I'm one of your few children who really loves this life, who really loves being in a body and walking around in this beautiful place you've created.

"But perhaps you think I might make a stronger point if I leave. Sometimes stories gain more strength than the people they were about. I don't know what the bigger vantage point is. I only know that I'm here because of you and that I will do as you want….and you seem to want this.

"I only ask that I go with as much grace and dignity as possible. So many brave men and women have prayed like this when faced with death by another's hand. Let me be brave as well."

The stars seemed to shimmer and sparkle a little more, as if in response to her request.

"Thank you."

She returned to the cottage and slipped into the warm bed beside her sister. In her dream that night she saw an island nation fall beneath the waves. Beautiful temples and palaces with columns and stairways with balustrades leading down to the ocean's side. Beautiful women and men walked the land and the cities with equal ease, in flowing, shimmering garments.

But something was amiss. Something was not right. Power, greed, corruption took over. And the island sank under the weight of its own vanity. The pain would continue in humanity.

Catriona awoke and sat up. She heard her father snoring. Elspeth moved in her sleep.

This was a time like that one—where fear and deceit was rampant. And like that other time of olde, humanity would continue….and we know that someday we'll get it right.

The man had been watching the house for hours, waiting for Catriona to emerge. Catriona thought he could wait a little longer. Hours longer. She fed the baby and busied herself with chores.

Finally Catriona walked down the walkway. The neighbors on either side of her cottage rushed into their homes.

It was just her…and him.

Elspeth opened the door with the baby in her arms and joined her sister.

"We're going to gather some herbs on the hillside," Catriona told the man. "Would you care to join us?"

He had obviously never been asked such a question, especially by someone he was investigating. His life was spent being shunned.

"Thank you," he stuttered. "That's kind of you. But no."

She and Elspeth walked up the path towards the meadows. After a few moments, she looked back. He was no longer in the pathway, but she knew he was watching still, from the shadows.

The two sisters dropped their baskets and then dropped themselves next to them. The baby started to fuss and, after scanning the hillside carefully to make certain the man and his lackey were not watching, she started to feed him. After just a few moments the baby was sound asleep, and she carefully set him down on a blanket.

The man was not going to leave, now that she had returned. Had part of her known he was awaiting her? Aye. And since he had set eyes on her, it seemed no one else would ever as greatly satisfy his…quota; his…penchant for the ghastly; his…twisted, stained sense of morality.

She had known her whole life that she wasn't going to live into her elder years. Perhaps it was the loss of her mother that made leaving seem easier.

Aye, she had known, but here it was — the end — right in front of her. She knew these men were on their fools' mission and took care of their business as quickly as possible. She also knew the village was under his spell, as so many villages fell under the cast of these men of the black cloth, with their wretched morals. Understanding and revering the very miracle of life was not part of their repertoire. Somehow they were able to weave their beliefs into the fabric of the communities they touched.

So here it was. A tremor passed through her and she shivered. Then she laughed. And then she started to cry.

She looked upward quickly, a movement she knew would stop the tears from flowing. She stared at the sky — the huge expanse of blue, like Elspeth's eyes, like her father's eyes. It matched her eyes, too, she'd often been told, but reflections in glass and water didn't reveal eyes that color to her so she had to take her admirers at their word.

She was lost in the expanse of the sky for a long while, a welcome respite from the pain. "Elspeth, can you imagine what's out there? Do you think it ever stops? It can't stop, because what would be on the other side? Just more of the same, perhaps, so it can't really stop, now can it?"

Elspeth took her sister's hand, but Catriona's babbling continued. "And what if we're not looking UP at the sky? What if we're looking DOWN? What if we're on the bottom of this sphere looking down into infinity instead of up into it?"

Elspeth kissed Catriona's hand and the babbling finally ceased.

Fear filled her entire body. She welcomed it as one might've welcomed a long-expected visitor. She let it course through her being, all levels — physical, emotional, etheric — until, quite a bit later, nigh on to an hour, it passed. That's all feelings want: to be felt. Then they move on. When they're not allowed that freedom, that's when they become stuck in aches and pains, excess weight, unwellness, even general misery.

"Oh my dear sister," Catriona whispered. "You're going to have to take the baby — all the time, alright? You would love to be able to play with him all the time, wouldn't you?"

To the question in Elspeth's eyes, Catriona continued. "I have to go, my love. Ouch!" She unclutched her sister's hand that had quickly clenched her arm.

"It would have been so much easier to just go, and not tell you I was going. But I could not do that to you. But you will be well. You have Father and the village and the baby. And I will be well, too." She saw Byron's smile through her tears. "I'll be meeting up with someone. Do you remember the handsome man who came to visit last spring? I'm going to see him again—isn't that grand?" She ran her fingers through Elspeth's curls. "And you will see me again, I promise you."

Elspeth curled up in Catriona's lap, in a tight, silent scream. Catriona held her sister until the baby awoke from his nap.

They were waiting for her by her cottage. No one else was in view. The two men escorted the women to the door and followed them inside. He pulled an instrument—a witch-pricker, they called it—from his garments and pricked Catriona's finger. It bled slightly, but he surreptitiously wiped the blood away and thrust her hand toward her father.

"No blood. She's on the side of the devil himself. Time to attend to her."

"Take the wee one, too?" The younger man reached for the baby, asleep in Elspeth's arms.

Catriona turned her back to the elder man and addressed the younger. "You take this child, and I will pull your useless, withered manhood out through your mouth."

"No, leave him."

The younger man concealed his sigh of relief from the elder. He was one of the ones in charge, though, so why did he cower at Catriona's threat?

Elspeth laid the babe in his tiny bed.

"Give me a moment," Catriona said to the men.

It was the only time in his life as a hunter he granted this request. He walked outside, pulling the young man with him.

Catriona turned to her sister. "Elspeth, as I told you, I have to leave you. I won't be coming back."

Elspeth clutched her hand.

"But I will see you again — in Heaven. I promise."

Perhaps the place of Heaven was made up to ease the grief of the living. The dead are fine — they're off on their new adventures. It's always harder on the ones left behind.

She brushed away Elspeth's tears which, although they had started only seconds before, were now streaming down her face.

"And every moment I can be by your side here, I will be."

She turned to her father and put her hands on each side of his face. "Father, I love you. I'll see you again, and every moment I can be by your side, too, there I will be."

Her father's face was blank, unseeing, unwilling to recognize what was happening. She kissed him and then walked over to the bed where her son lay sleeping. She gently ran her finger over his face and down to his heart.

"My beloved son, I know there's a way to be with you still, because my own mother has never left me. I will be by your side for every moment of your life, and even onward after — forever."

96

CHAPTER 8

She walked outside. No one else was in the pathways, but she could feel them watching. She and the man walked to the empty dwelling where he had been living for the last weeks.

Once her eyes got accustomed to the gloom inside, she could see a table set out. Chains with handcuffs were hammered into the four corners of the table. The only other item of furniture in the room was a stool. There was a whip and a fire poker by the fire.

Catriona lay down on the table.

No one, in his experience, had ever done that without force and severe pain applied to her.

"What is it that you fear?"

That was supposed to be his question.

"I fear nothing." And before she could ask another question, he quickly queried, "What is it that you fear?"

"Nothing." She paused; he waited for her to continue. "Sir, no loving parent would have some for just a few of the children and none for the others. There is enough, more than enough."

He picked up a whip that was lying near the table. "How, if you're so all-knowing and powerful, could you let this be happening to you?"

"Why wouldn't God love a child just as a parent would love a child? If you believe in a God of suffering and retribution, no wonder you're suffering."

The whip crashed across her face, taking her breath away. Before her stunned skin could even respond to the pain, she asked, "Don't you know who you are?" She let him be silent for a moment. "I didn't think so. If you did, you wouldn't be doing this."

He slapped the whip across her face again and she passed out. He tried to revive her but to no avail.

She slowly opened her eyes. She couldn't tell what that dark apparition was, right in front of her face.

"Welcome back. We've been waiting for you," he said.

Four hands—although it felt like more—groped at her most private parts, ripping her clothes away. That was enough. As during that time once before, she willed her spirit to leave her body.

The man looked into her eyes and realized that she had left. He whipped the limp form on the table, in a frenzied attempt to bring her back.

As Catriona watched from the other side of the room, the spirit of the man turned to her and came to her side. They regarded each other for a long while.

"I had to," he said.

"No, you didn't," she replied.

"We set it up this way. Long ago. Do you not remember?"

"Yes. I was to help you forgive yourself."

He thought for a long moment after the surprise left his face. "Yes."

An hour later, she returned to her body. "I would think you would have learned the lesson from Jesus's death," she whispered to them.

"You have the audacity to compare yourself with our Lord?"

"I think he would think you're the audacious one, to not put yourself where he was. Why would our infinite creator give us an example of how to live that we could not attain?"

"Comparing yourself to Jesus! You must be out of your mind with pain and torment, from what you've done."

Rats scurried across the floor. Two of the three cringed; one welcomed her animal companion.

"Didn't your good book say that Jesus said be ye as Gods? All the bad people go to Heaven. That's where we all meet to decide how we'll help each other be all that we can."

"You're addled, woman."

"There is no Hell. There is only Heaven after this, and I'll be meeting you there."

"You're delirious."

"And it would be my honor."

He handed the whip to his young accomplice and reached for the fire poker. Too tired and horrified to will her spirit out of her body once again, she gratefully passed out.

When she awoke, she heard him talking to her as if from miles away.

"You make a horrid sinne. You take a weakness for superstition and cast your spells upon it. What you call healing is a sinne." The blazing fire cast strange shadows, which danced on his face, making his eyes glow horrifically, then disappear, glow again, then disappear yet again.

"Did not Jesus heal?" she whispered.

"But he was God. God can heal."

"You say God is our Father. Would not a parent pass their most prized attribute on to their children? Would not our creator give the same unto us?"

"You're a froward creature. This is your last night on earth, lass. Make your peace with God."

"I know you're loving somewhere deep inside." She paused for a moment, sensing another presence in the room, although he wasn't physically there. "You love a man. He loves you, too."

Catriona didn't see the closed fist swinging at the side of her head. She only saw the expression on the younger man as he regarded his mentor with surprise, which quickly turned to confusion, then to revulsion. Blackness came.

When she awoke, she wasn't certain if the room was so pitch from the arrival of night or if the excruciating, pounding injury on the side of her head had caused her eyesight to fail. The throbbing brought dizziness, which resulted in a feeling of falling deeper into the darkness. She could feel that more torment had been wreaked upon her body until they realized that no amount of additional pain was going to rouse her.

She heard a rustle, which alerted her to the presence of her...well, perhaps others would call them her tormenters, but even in this state of severe pain and confusion, she would not have, had she been able to speak. She did not move even a finger, however, for although she did not despise them, there was no need to let them know she was awake.

As her eyes grew accustomed to the dark surroundings, she could see their outlines against the dying embers of the hearth. They weren't asleep. Rats again scurried in the corner of the room, however, which made them squirm a bit. They looked in her direction, but she'd already shut her eyes.

She could hear the whispering—beings filled the room, but from another dimension. It was a low din, as if thousands were speaking softly to her. The buzz comforted her.

This time, she whispered back, inside her head. *Beloved Life, I don't know why you're allowing your children to be taken in this manner. Healing is not a grievous sinne. Magick is not cavorting with the devil. But I know it's not you who call this; I know it's fearful, confused people...who think they are acting in your name.*

Although she had known her time was coming, she'd still clasped the essence of holding on to her life. Whether it was the extreme pain or the dizziness muddling her thoughts or something else, in that moment came her surrender.

Creator of us all, I give thee my life. Just let me be brave. Let it be swift. Let the pain pass beyond my body. Let me be with you. We've always been together, I know. Let me be one with you quickly.

She'd never been afraid to die, perhaps because she lived between the veils anyway—one foot in the human world and the other in the spirit world. She wasn't even afraid of the pain of the method of how she would die. Her heart ached, though, for her son, for her sister, for her father. She knew how close they were to the other side, the one beyond the veil. But they didn't.

She knew she would watch her son grow to manhood, marry, have children, die as an old man surrounded by generations of children. But he didn't know that. Just as her own mother did, she would whisper to him during the between times—the times of falling asleep and just waking up, when the human mind is most susceptible to listening...and hearing...and remembering...and knowing...and....

SECTION FOUR

FIRE

CHAPTER 9

I killed her. Even with all the perspective this side gives, I'm still so deeply ashamed. Even though I left the physical long ago, my heart still aches. There's a hole in my etheric being—where my heart would be—

How…could…we?

How…do…we…still?

When will we learn? And stop this madness that still continues?

The tumbrel creaked and moaned as our village's one horse slowly pulled it up the hillside. We townsfolk followed, without quite knowing what we were doing or what was happening. Hiding from oneself is how humanity survived so long.

We could hardly look at her. Even with her face beaten and bruised and her hair looking not fit to house vermin, she was still….lovely.

Our beautiful hillsides, normally a lush emerald green, were amber that spring. The rains had stopped. The despicable younger man had cleared away a…stage, is what it seemed like. In the center of the large circle of bare dirt stood a post surrounded by twigs. Rocks surrounded the outer rim of the circle. He obviously had great strength, which was all the more surprising given his small stature. His hatred must've been what gave him the strength to move the many large rocks.

This is the part I don't want to write about. How can I describe a burning at the stake? And why should I have to? How could the heart of a human create such a thing? How could the same heart that can crack open in ecstasy also create devices of torture? Oh, what humans have done to each other. And the biggest crime of all is doing it in the name of God.

How can we let you know what it's like to feel the flesh burn on your body…to smell the burning flesh…to feel the searing of your own skin…to know that your own end is coming?

Catriona was able to bring herself out of this pain. Not so with millions of others in the burning times who had to feel the excruciating pain of their flesh melting on their bodies.

Oh, how can we do such things to each other? It's one thing to take the liberty of snuffing the life of another. That is perverse in and of itself. But to prolong the agony? That's even worse.

The witch hunter was doing it to himself. We can't do anything to another that we're not doing to ourselves.

He thought he was right. And Catriona was right about him. Somehow in the dark recesses of his mind, he thought he was doing the right thing — for himself, for his country, for his God. We take a little boy whose father died young and his mother took her pain out on her oldest son, the future witch-hunter. She was crazed with grief for many years, 'til he was practically grown. By then it was too late; the harm had been inflicted by her mental instability.

He found a welcoming home within the fortress of the church. He even found welcoming arms there, and welcome warmth and sexuality, which he'd never experienced before. But of course that could not be mentioned. In fact he never fully owned this part of him, not even inside his own head. This abomination was a sinne upon a sinne upon a sinne. Not even his dim awareness of the extent that this sinne was carried out in his monastery and others throughout the entire region could assuage his unspoken, unuttered guilt.

So this burning shame turned outward—especially toward the all-powerful women who represented his mother. Their wails of pain was his own pain expressed, so it eased it a bit. But of course what they were doing was a crime against their own nature, so the pain came back a hundredfold. They didn't understand the source—that they were the source of their magnified pain—so they did it again.

And yet, his Creator loves him, too. Source loves him like Source loves everything everywhere in Its creation. The dilemma was that this beloved being's own love did not include himself—in fact, he regarded himself as reprehensible…so he had to inflict pain.

Aye, he lived in so much pain of his own making, that he had to create that pain in others—not to mask his own, but to compete with it, to challenge it, to bring it out.

And we let him. To her. Our golden child.

Earth is a young planet.

The two men placed her in the middle of the wood and tied her hands behind the stake. The disgusting little man lit the fire, and the townspeople stepped back as the twigs were engulfed in flames.

Witch hunters had devious ways to keep their prey from passing out, so they would feel more pain. But somehow these two knew not to even bother, except with the small size of the fire.

What must go through someone's head as they take the life of another? What must go through someone's head as they watch someone take the life of another? Sometimes the answer is surprising: absolutely nothing. The whole town watched her die. We were stunned, shocked. Absolutely nothing of any coherence went through our heads. Someone noticed a lark singing in the field. Another noticed a wispy cloud in the cobalt-blue sky.

It would be a while before the reality of that afternoon set in. We let it happen. We let a stranger come to our village and dictate his strange social mores on us. How could we have let that happen?

As I mentioned, the fire the young man set was small. It was that way by design, for if the fire was too large the victim would die quickly of taking smoke into the lungs and suffocating.

Maira seemed to shake herself and come to her senses. It was too late to save her friend, but at least she could save her from the extra pain of a slow death. She started to throw more twigs and wood on the fire.

"No, you must not do that," the old man shouted at her.

"You better dare not stop me."

Her courage gave us others courage, and many of us threw more twigs and small logs on the fire. Why did we find our courage then and not before the first twig was set alight? Or even before he took her from her home? Or even when he first came down the mountainside and into our village?

After looking at us all one by one, Catriona left her body. The man poked her, trying to bring her back so that she would feel the pain, but she hovered above her physical form.

For one moment, she went back into her body and looked at him. Oh, how she looked at him! Never was so much love, compassion, forgiveness bestowed on an executioner. He almost stumbled.

She looked beyond the circle and smiled—I knew she could see Byron standing on the edge, smiling back at her, warmly welcoming her to the other side.

Then she left her body for good as her form succumbed to the flames.

The man stared at the form disappearing in the roar of the fire.

"Do you want to gather up any more?" the young toady asked his mentor. "I know her friends must also be—"

"No," he answered, far more quietly than was usual for him. "That should do it for now." He left the circle.

Catriona's spirit started to float upward, but she reversed direction and floated to her father's side.

"Father, I know you tried. You were doing the best you could. I love you. I'll love you forever."

The old man looked at the black figure rushing up the hillside. For a moment his stooped frame regained some of its strength and stature from years earlier.

"You don't have to go after him," Catriona whispered. "Life exacts its own."

Elspeth stared at the flames as they started to subside. She had no thoughts in her mind at all — she was in shock.

"Elspeth, my love," Catriona whispered in her ear, "I'm not in the embers. I'm here, right beside you."

Elspeth shook herself and looked around her in confusion.

"You will be well, my dear sister. All is well. Time here is so fleeting, really. I will see you again, and sooner than you know."

Catriona placed a gentle kiss on her sister's cheek. Elspeth raised her hand to her face and rubbed her cheek.

"Take good care of my baby, now your baby. I love you. That will never, ever change." Catriona brushed her etheric fingers down the side of her baby's face. And then she disappeared to the eternal realms.

Elspeth turned from the fire. A nearby man put his arm out to her.

"Don't you dare touch me," she hissed at him. She wrapped her shawl around the baby and left the circle, leaving the townspeople with their mouths agape.

"She speaks!"

"Did you hear that?"

On the ridge, heading up the mountainside, the figure in black hurried away. The smaller figure remained close to his heels, like a dog.

Somewhere on the other side of the mountain he stopped short, and the smaller figure bumped into him. The old man started to speak, then stopped. His face was......empty. Blank. The old man seemed as mystified by this blankness as the younger man was.

"Sir?"

"Not now." He sat down on a nearby rock, looking off into the distance. He tried to find some semblance of his self, but the inside of him seemed to be empty.

He looked at the vista of the rest of his life, empty now without this mission that had consumed him for so long. What would he do? Where would he go?

"Anywhere you want," Catriona whispered to him. "Anything is possible."

Anyone observing from a distance would see an old man bolt from his seat on a rock. The young man tried to follow him, but the old man pushed him away. As he careened down the mountainside, the limp in his leg seemed to ease.

But then he fell to the ground, heaving and screaming, clawing at the earth. Souls screaming at the gates of Hell —if there was such a thing—wouldn't have sounded near as mournful.

This was his last formal act in his office. He was relieved of his duties by himself, by committing suicide. The last witch was burned in Scotland about one hundred and twenty-five years later and the act allowing such atrocities was ended just under a decade afterward.

Several hours after the man left, Maira, too, stumbled up the mountainside. The village could hear her howls of rage and, more than once, a plaintive, "Why?"

When we ask "Why?" the universe will answer us. It will show us our parts in the creation of whatever has happened. Most of us don't want—can't bear—to see our parts, however.

To some, Maira's cries on the hillside were harder to bear than Catriona's burning. Sometimes a soothing balm of shock settles over someone when they have to endure the unendurable, like watching a woman devoted to a life of love and light burn as a symbol of hate and darkness before your very eyes. But the numbness was starting to wear off, just a tad, though, when Maira's cries were carried to us by the wind.

All work in the village ground to a halt. As twilight came, no fires were started for the evening meal. The shock was starting to wear off. And in the moments when our hearts would let us actually sense what they were still trying to deny, as when we heard Maira, we were so, so ashamed.

Later that night, there was a scream, a wail, a keening. It started low and grew more and more shrill. Everyone in town stumbled out of our cottages and peered into the night for the source of the sound.

It came from Catriona's cottage. Shane yanked open the door to find Elspeth in the middle of the floor, screaming and screaming and screaming. The screams broke off sharply as she took a deep inhale only to let the howl continue. Miraculously, the baby slept.

After nearly an hour of screaming she spoke. She looked at the small crowd gathered in her doorway. "You killed her! You killed her! How could you!"

The miracle of hearing her voice in the screams overpowered the pain in what she said. No one said a word.

"I did it, too. I let it happen, too."

The townswomen held her. Her sobs subsided to a whimper, and finally she fell asleep in Aileen's arms.

Elspeth was still as light and frail as a bird. Aileen picked her up and placed her gently on the bed. The streak in the eastern sky let us know that morning was not far away.

Catriona came to Elspeth in her dreams, offering her flowers. She had a lamb, as well.

"I thought you were dead," Elspeth said to her sister in her dream.

"No, my darling sister, I'm right here, right by your side," Catriona said, softly stroking her hair. "Where I've always been and where I'll always be."

When Elspeth awoke, she thought she saw her sister standing over the sleeping baby. When she rubbed the sleep out of her eyes, the apparition had disappeared. She rubbed her eyes again. The baby was sleeping peacefully. But it wasn't an apparition—she knew her sister had been there.

"The veils are very thin," she heard Catriona whisper. "Much thinner than most on Earth realize. Everywhere there are helpers, seers, trying to guide you along. Just listen."

SECTION FIVE

LOVE,
THE FIFTH ELEMENT

116

By this time you well know what I'm going to say, just like the other four. Aye, I killed her, too. We all did—just by not saying no to one man on a fool's errand.

This could've been written by all ninety-two of us, because we all let it happen.

Late that next morning, we gathered in the square circle. Just saying that silly name all these centuries later still makes me smile.

Maira said it first. "I dreamed of Catriona last night. I saw her with Byron."

"You saw them, too?" Aileen asked. "Aye, I saw that as well. Dancing, they were."

"Aye, I saw that, too."

"Aye—"

Luckily, instead of the horror of seeing someone we treasured disintegrate into ash and embers, we were forever able to remember her dancing with her true love. I think that was a gift she came that night to give to each one of us. Well, that's what I'd like to believe, so I'll go with that.

As we've said, she wasn't a saint or anything like that. I don't know how she did it. While most of us just went about our daily routine with a grumble here and there, she would find something new with every chore, on her hundredth walk to the creek, her thousandth time milking her cow. I don't know how she came in this way.

She seemed to have a special relationship with....everything. The wind. The rain. The entire village would be grumbling about the fourth straight day of rain and Catriona would be out spinning pirouettes in it. And the raindrops seemed to spin pirouettes back around her. The winds through the tall grasses seemed to wave at her....and of course she'd wave back.

Aye, we'd see a dreary, rainy day and she'd see.....something else. We'd see a dreary, work-filled life and she'd see....something else. She garnered her strength from the ground, her laughter from wind, her passion from the sun, her flexibility from the rains.

We weren't sure if she was right in the head, you know. As we watched her grow up, so happy and all, we looked for signs that she wasn't all there, you see. But there weren't any such signs...just the happiest lass you ever saw.

So how an entire village could let their golden lass be...

Oh, even from this side of the veil and from this perspective, it's hard to say. Fear can spread like a plague and put a tight grasp on otherwise intelligent people's hearts. Our beloved God, Jesus — at least that's who some of us thought he was back then — had the same thing happened when he died, I imagine. Otherwise sensible people can turn into an angry mob, with an angry mob mentality. And it happened over and over and over again. It still does.

But Catriona took her death with as much grace as she lived her life. And, thankfully, she also knew how to leave her body.

I think we just haven't understood for so long. We have no idea that the universe is comprised of love and light, let alone that that's what we're made of, too. We come of age on this planet to parents who have come of age with no lessons in life. For so long we thought it was just about getting through the day, herding the sheep, providing for the family.

And yet....there are the pyramids. There's Stonehenge. There are tributes to something greater.

But every human—every single human being—knows that yearning for more. We have a hunger that food will not appease, a thirst that no drink can quench, a physical longing that no amount of touch can satisfy. And it's probably that longing that drives people crazy. It might be that very longing that drove the men of the church to fabricate such lies and perform such atrocities in the name of.......God?! In the name of a man who stood for love and peace and compassion.....? Good God, have we gone stark raving mad?

Yes.

Yes, we have.

And the madness would be even greater if we let it continue.

Aye, her life was taken so soon. Oh, but she lived more life than the rest of us in the village lived, put together. She could see more life in the palm of her hand, in one bright flash of afternoon sunshine, than many of us see in a year, in a lifetime. She saw the miracle that is this very life.

Why didn't she run? Why didn't she hide? Why did we do nothing to stop it all? There was nothing preventing us from cornering him and putting him in the very prison he had created.

Perhaps she spoke even louder to us through her death than through her life. Maybe it's more in the remembering of her that we take pause. Oh, yes, we took pause every time we saw her, every time we heard her laugh carried on the wind, every time she looked at us. But she lived in our hearts even more after she left.

I don't know how it happened, how we let it happen, but we did. She was our favorite daughter, our village loved one, and we let this happen to her. I can't explain it; none of us can.

The man came with the power of a faraway, untouchable fortress at his back. We reckoned that the Church had some good things to say, but its words seemed far away from our green hills. He came to our village spouting those truths, as he called them, but they were far from truths. They were words of confusion. They were lies.

"Repent, and ye will be saved," he said.

Well, at this point I've met John the Baptist and that's not what he said at all. "Turn toward the truth," is what he said.

"Repent, turn your life over to the savior, there is none other than our Lord Jesus Christ."

Well, at this point, I've met Jesus too. We all have. And let me tell you, he's shaking his head at that whole notion, he is!

He came to teach about the inner divinity, to follow your own inner authority. And the Church completely turned that around and made it the external authority in so many people's lives. Jesus certainly didn't want anyone to fight in his name, kill in his name. What about when he said, "They will know you by how you love one another, not by how you worship me." Aye?

And there this man was, coming to our village in Jesus's name, and taking our favorite from us. He came with a cloud of darkness around him. The cloud expanded until the entire lot of us was in the darkness with him. And it called to the darkest inside us. It happened because he said there would be others after him if we gave him any trouble — that the whole town would be taken if anyone dissented with his authority.

It wasn't long after that the hunts for witches started to fade away. They were relegated to just another atrocity that humanity has inflicted upon humanity.

And yet they continue, in one form or another, even now, by people in as much pain and confusion as the witch hunters. Let us allow them all to fade away.

Someday there will be a return to the inner authority — not the small ego who thinks it's in charge of everything. It flits about from here to there and back again, half crazed, thinking time is running out, thinking this must happen or that must happen, thinking there's not enough love to go around. Aye, small only sees small.

There's not enough time unless and until we understand that time is all there is. Time doesn't run out. It's all we have. All of it. It never ends. And we will always be here. Wherever here is. Whoever or whatever we are.

There's not enough love to go around unless and until we understand that love is all there is, too. Love is all there is. It belongs to all of us — all of it, all of us. It never ends. And it will always be here. Truly, it's all there is.

It was because of me that she died. At least that's what I thought then. But I know now that she died because it was a product of those times.

And who was the main storyteller here, here in this last section? Who am I? Can you guess?

I'm the person who loved her the most, even more than Byron.

Am I Maira? Byron? Aileen? Shane?

Nay. Maira told you of Earth. Aileen told you of Water. Shane told you of Air. Edward told you of Fire. And I'm speaking now. I'm with her again, even now. And I'm still her sister.

I didn't speak because I didn't want to. Living with Catriona was like being in a constant meditation of life. Words would have dispelled the magical, mystical feeling of time with her. I just wanted to hear her talk, hear her voice and the cadence of her words, have her tones transport me to other dimensions. I relished my silence because it brought her being into higher volume; hence my life was lived at a much higher level.

Also, though, it was if I always knew she was going to be taken from me, and that knowledge compressed my spirit so much that I could hardly speak. Once it finally happened, once she was taken from me, the thing I'd been dreading my whole life was finished. Nothing could be worse, so there was nothing more to fear.

But, truth is, she never left me. I felt her by my side for all the rest of my days, reminding me of the colors and the sparks and the endless joys of life.

And that magnificent son of hers, whom I raised as my own? Aye, he went on to be a man of power and impact. But he will most probably tell you his story on his own someday.

For so many humans, we're remembered more when we're dead than appreciated while we're alive. We notice what we're missing instead of what we have. The sun has an added allure, nay perhaps a mystique, on a cloudy day, but do we relish it when it's warming our face? Aye, some do. She did.

Love him and her and them while they're here. It can be a long, lonely time without them.

We killed her. The people who loved her. Her village. Her family and loved ones. The ones she let know were the biggest gift of her life, the most radiant beings anywhere. We all killed her. We all let her die. Somehow we didn't say anything. Why did we do that? Why did they allow Jesus to die? Or Galileo? Or anyone, anytime, ever?

Everything works for its time. Everything is the best we can be doing for the time. And mine was a time when we didn't know any better. We were acting like little children who needed the stern, long arm of the Church to take us by the scruff of the neck and set us aright. But what kind of aright were we talking about? Ach, perhaps we needed the great myths of Heaven and Hell to put enough fear in us to behave, to work hard for that distant day when we'll all meet in Paradise.

But Catriona's idea of Paradise was.....now! Or then, as it were.

It's actually an ingenious design. To allow us all to come here to....what? To awaken. How would you design the world? How would you get people to awaken their compassion? Would you do it any differently?

God so loved the world....

That God, Life, sent us all here.

Such a life. Such a time. Such......pain. Such......love. Such. .....tragedy. The ones who died are such heroes. So are the ones who lived....and live....then and now.

While the rest of us were wearing hair shirts and flagellating ourselves for some sinne we hadn't even committed, she had somehow exonerated herself from the guilt that plagues the human race. She just made that choice at a very early age, like we all can. We can't choose what happens to us necessarily, although to some extent we can, but we can choose our reactions. And everything she did supported her choice to live full out, enjoy, as the sunshine lights up the day.

She's with us now. We're with you now. We're back there now, here and there. We're everywhere, just like you are. Part of the magic is to see beyond the veil while the veil is up. What you can do is so much more than what we can do — we see more, but it's not a fair contest. We're on top of the mountain, so of course we can see far distances. You're down in the valley. But if you let yourself see eternity, while you're in the mortal flesh, that's a contest well won.

We can be such a confused lot, we human creatures, especially when the creature part of us meets the higher part of us, who tells us what could be. We don't know how to do it—even if that higher part is right in front of us showing us, clearly, with every word, every step, every deed. Well, almost every deed.

At the same time, humans have so much wisdom. Perhaps those of us beyond the veil have higher wisdom…we have a higher perspective, anyway. But you're the ones walking around the planet in a body. The job is to live this wisdom while in that beautiful body you've been given.

We're all equal. No one is better than another. It's just that some are awake to the majesty within; most aren't. That's the whole design—to awaken to the majesty that is within, without, everywhere. In that place, there can be no war, no witch hunting, just peace, generosity. We can know who we are. And when we know who we are, we know who everyone else is, too.

And once we awaken and train ourselves to stay in that state, everything falls into its right place. Everything.

We are all one. Just like every drop of water has the same properties as the mighty ocean, so are we one with the whole of the cosmos. We just don't have the point of view of the mighty ocean, the whole of the cosmos. But we are connected with it.

The game is to progress, here on earth. The other realms are watching, waiting. When humanity does finally grasp it, there will be a glorious celebration that will echo to the far reaches of the cosmos.

And yet, it doesn't have to be a struggle. We don't need more martyrs down through the ages. Just simple tasks done with great love will do it. You don't have to save the whole world, but lifting up everything you do will save your own world....which will lift up the whole world...and the whole universe. Love more....with every breath, every blink, every word, every action, aye, even every bite and sip.

Are you saving the world and killing yourself with poor habits and unpleasantness coursing through your mind? Don't do us all any favors. Save yourself first: Be happy. Do what you love. Just love your spouse. Allow your hands to give and receive love to and from the earth as you plant your seedlings. Love your children—let them know who they are and help them awaken. That will serve us more than anything.

A civilized person would not think of hurting anything, let alone a fellow human being. But civilized is not always how we characterize people. And I can say this: because when I was there during Catriona's time, I was as bad as the witch hunter. I didn't say anything. That makes me culpable.

What are you not saying?

On the other hand, it's all right. We can't get it wrong. We have eternity. We're all on a steady progression upward.

Perhaps it's all a game, a theater. When the witch hunters died, they were as welcomed to the life beyond life as the witches were. When Jesus' executors died, they were as welcomed as he was. As Catriona told our father, Life exacts its own. So they were welcomed, but they had to live what returns to those who act as they did.

If you know these things now, in this moment, why not do it now? Even though we can't get it wrong, that doesn't mean we shouldn't get it right…right now.

We were better for her being here, even if her stay was cut short. The world is always better for just one person being here. That person is you.

THE END

Ann Crawford

AFTERWORD

I remember this life like it was an hour ago. Fragments of it have come to me over the years. No one knows absolutely for sure if we have been here before, how many lives we have lived here, but many of us sense it strongly.

I'm just scratching the surface of what Catriona came in knowing. I asked a friend who is an intuitive if it's possible to go backward so much! She assured me that we eternal souls—and that's every one of us, by the way—are not necessarily on a linear path.

I love my four siblings dearly….and that's quite something considering how we light up the full spectrum of far right to far left politically, from very religious to not so much. But there was one I had a special affinity with.

My mother was very sick from before I was born, and my sister Betsey was my primary caregiver for my early years. After Mom died when I was still a teenager, Betsey was my big sister and surrogate mom.

One time Betsey and I were driving along a road in rural Kansas (both of us tend to get off the beaten path some). She mentioned to me she remembered being my sister in another life, and something happened to me, but she couldn't help me. The girl that she once was would come to her in visions, still upset. She assured her that she'd made up for it in this life—that she'd taken really, really good care of me.

By this time I had tears slipping down my face. I pulled the car over to the side of the road and looked at her. I told her I was writing a book about a woman who was killed during the Burning Times, and she had a sister she had to leave.

We were both sobbing by this point and held each other tightly. Time and space and miles and memories brought us together and helped us remember…and finish what was started before. Love does that—finishes what It started.

Is that memory real? Does it matter? It lives in us nevertheless.

We carry so many memories in us. The first time I was underwater and heard the high-pitched call of a dolphin, I remembered that sound from eons ago, from across time, even from across space, perhaps. Catriona might not have been an earlier rendition of me, but she lives in me, and I carry her in me along with so many others. May her—and my, and your—love and light and joy live forever.

In loving memory and honor
of all those
persecuted and killed
by people who were confused
and didn't understand.

Ann Crawford

ACKNOWLEDGEMENTS

Betsey, Perry, Susan, Connie,
and Mom and Dad

Barbara Cox
Veronica Entwistle
Frances Mary Frane
Rev. Karyl Huntley
Lavandar
Ashanta Lipari
Rev. Lee McNeil Nash
Angela Melia
Sherry Robb
Janet Carol Ryan
Grace Sears
Dana Swift
Samantha White
Lisa and Kathy
Marion
Jim Self, Roxanne Burnett, and the MA Players
Joan and John Walker
Alysa Sanzari-Hall for the beautiful book cover

Last of my acknowledgements,

but first in my life, my beloved Steve —
my rock, my love, my best friend,
the love of my life.

Ann Crawford

Books by Ann Crawford

Available in paperback, e-book,
and audiobook versions

Life in the Hollywood Lane

Spellweaver

*Angels on Overtime —
a heartwarming love story of angelic proportions*

*Mary's Message —
The Story of Mary Magdalene and Yeshua ben Yosef*

*Visioning —
Creating the Life of Our Dreams and a
World that Works for Us All*

To follow Ann's blog,
please visit anncrawford.net.
To inquire about Ann speaking to your
book club or group, please contact
info@lightscapespublishing.com.